"A seduction is not just a seduction."

He continued to whisper into the phone receiver. "It's different for everyone. What turns one woman on may turn you off completely."

"I suppose that's true." Erin laughed. "I don't care much for leather and chains."

It was too easy to imagine himself seducing this woman he'd never seen. Laughing, he tried to ignore his body's reaction to the suggestive conversation. "So, what would turn you on?"

"I guess I'm pretty traditional," she said shyly. "Flowers, soft music, a crackling fire."

He'd half expected that. He already knew she was quite traditional in some ways. "Okay, what else? What about the actual lovemaking? You like it slow and easy? Hot and rough? Do you like to make love once and go to sleep, or keep at it all night long?"

"Stop," Erin moaned with embarrassment. "I can't deal with this."

"Turning you on?" Turned on himself, he squirmed restlessly in his chair. "Just imagine what it'll be like if you'd only agree to meet me...."

Several years ago, **Gina Wilkins** heard a "stranger-than-fiction" story from a co-worker. This woman had had a twenty-minute conversation with a man who she assumed was her father. Finally, they both figured out that he had dialed the wrong number and was talking to someone else's daughter. And what was even more bizarre, his daughter worked in the same place as they did! This amusing incident stayed with Gina, and she toyed with the idea of turning it into a romance. The result was *Hotline*. Gina found it both fun and a challenge to write a romance that evolves through a series of telephone conversations!

Books by Gina Wilkins

HARLEQUIN TEMPTATION
283—COULD IT BE MAGIC
299—CHANGING THE RULES
309—AFTER HOURS
337—A REBEL AT HEART
353—A PERFECT STRANGER

Don't miss any of our special offers. Write to us at the following address for information on our newest releases.

Harlequin Reader Service
P.O. Box 1397, Buffalo, NY 14240
Canadian address: P.O. Box 603,
Fort Erie, Ont. L2A 5X3

Hotline
GINA WILKINS

Harlequin Books

TORONTO • NEW YORK • LONDON
AMSTERDAM • PARIS • SYDNEY • HAMBURG
STOCKHOLM • ATHENS • TOKYO • MILAN

Published November 1991

ISBN 0-373-25469-5

HOTLINE

1

THE ANTIQUE LAMP on the bedside table cast a soft amber glow across the Queen Anne bedroom furniture. Listening to the low rumble of thunder, Erin pulled her ballet-length nightgown over her head. She smoothed it over her slender hips, observing her image in the cheval mirror across the room. Erin knew she was considered beautiful—shapely, dark-haired, blue-eyed, delicately featured. Still, no one waited in the empty bed behind her; no one would step out of the adjoining bath to catch his breath in appreciation of the sight of her clad in thin, lace-trimmed silk.

Suppressing a sigh, Erin turned away from the mirror and brushed a strand of hair from her mouth, dreaming of a fantasy lover who would hold her, laugh with her, share the summer storm with her. . . .

The telephone rang at almost the same moment thunder crashed loudly enough to rattle the doors and windows. She wasn't even certain she'd heard the phone until it rang again. With one eye on the open bedroom door across the hall, Erin snatched up the receiver, surprised the deafening boom hadn't woken Chelsea.

"Sis?" The voice was muffled by noisy static.

Erin smiled in pleasure at the call from her older brother. "This connection is terrible," she said, raising her voice. "Can you hear me?"

"Yeah. Am *I* coming through?"

Hotline

"Yes. And it's about time you called! I was starting to worry. You sound kind of funny, though. Are you all right?"

"I've got a lousy cold," he answered glumly. "I could hardly talk at all, yesterday."

She reacted with characteristic worry. "Have you taken anything for it? Have you seen a doctor?"

"No, 'Mommy,' I haven't seen a doctor," he answered teasingly. "It's only a cold. Modern medicine hasn't discovered a cure, remember?"

"Sorry. I guess you're getting all the smothering care you need from the girlfriend." Erin tried not to sound too disdainful. Adam knew exactly how she felt about his latest inamorata. There was no need to start another quarrel about her.

After only a brief pause, he replied flatly. "That's over. She's history."

"Really?" Erin hoped she didn't sound too thrilled. Twirling a strand of her shoulder-length hair around one finger, she tried to sound nonchalant when she asked, "What happened?"

"Long story. Suffice it to say I finally saw beneath the pretty exterior and discovered that the interior wasn't nearly as attractive."

"Isn't that exactly what I told you?" she couldn't resist murmuring, not sure he'd hear her over the static.

He did. "No I-told-you-so's right now, okay? I'm sick and alone and tired. Save it until I'm in better shape to defend myself."

She rolled her eyes at the obvious play for sympathy. "All right, but the minute you're better . . ."

He laughed rather hoarsely. "I'll start practicing being defensive as soon as I hang up. You know, you sound a little strange, yourself. *You're* not coming down with something, are you?"

Erin shook her head, forgetting he couldn't actually see her. "Just tired, I guess. Long day at the grindstone."

"You're not overdoing it, are you? I've always said you try to do too much at once. You need to slow down, take some time to relax."

She frowned a bit, straining to hear him. Funny, he didn't sound at all like himself. That cold really must be a bad one. "I'm okay, really. I'm glad you called. I've missed talking to you. Especially now that Corey's moved off to the Ozarks to find herself, or some such nonsense. The two of you are the only ones who really understand my weird sense of humor."

A series of annoying pops made her wince and hold the receiver a few inches from her ear.

"*Who* moved away?" he asked when the noise faded.

"Corey," she repeated more clearly, wondering why he'd had to ask. "Come on, Adam, the cold hasn't affected your memory, has it? I mean, Corey's only my best friend, as you well know. I talk about her all the time."

"Honey, I'm sorry, but who—? Wait a minute. *Adam?*"

Confused, Erin began to worry that the cold really *was* affecting his mind. Could he be feverish? "What's wrong?"

"I thought you called me Adam," he explained during a respite on the phone line. The static on the line gradually lessened as the storm abated. His voice, hoarse from his cold, was clear—and not at all familiar! "Now, start over, Cheryl. Who's Corey? I honestly don't remember you mentioning her before."

Erin frowned. "*Cheryl?*" she repeated, tightening her grip on the receiver.

There was a moment of blank silence—and then: "This *is* Cheryl, isn't it?"

"No. You mean—you're not Adam?"

The voice on the other end of the line groaned. "Oh, boy. I'm really sorry. I must have gotten a wrong number. I thought you were my sister."

Even though he couldn't see her, Erin hid her flaming face with her free hand. "I thought you were my brother!"

His low laugh made her smile weakly despite herself. "Did I even get the right city? I was *trying* to call North Little Rock, Arkansas—555-2026."

"Well, you got the right city," Erin answered lightly. "But my number's 555-2029. You hit the wrong button."

He laughed again. "Talk about strange... I really thought you were Cheryl."

"And I really thought you were Adam," she repeated, her smile widening a bit. *How ridiculous!* The guys at the ad agency would love this one! Not that they'd ever believe it, she decided, chuckling.

"I don't suppose your brother lives in Boston, does he?" he asked, obviously amused. "Now that *would* be a wild coincidence."

"No, Adam's in California—most of the time. He travels a lot." But he wouldn't care about that, she told herself quickly. He was calling long-distance, and he wanted to talk to his sister. "Maybe you can get a refund on your call if you explain what happened to the operator," she suggested.

"Yeah." He didn't sound as though he cared one way or the other about the cost. "I guess you'd still like to hear from your brother, wouldn't you? Are you really anxious about him?"

Touched by his question, she responded reassuringly. "Oh, I'm sure he'll turn up soon. He does this sometimes."

"The Corey who's living in a cabin in the Ozarks—you said she's your friend?" It seemed as if he wanted to prolong the call. Strangely enough, so did she.

"Yes—my best friend," she answered. Even as she said the words, she realized what an understatement they were. Corey had been wonderful during Erin's divorce four years earlier, standing by her when others had drifted away. Most of the people she'd known during her marriage had been Martin's friends; and somehow, after the divorce, he'd retained custody of them. He'd wanted his friends—it had been his wife and daughter he considered inconveniences.

Since her divorce, Erin had been busy rebuilding her life—finding work as a free-lance illustrator, taking care of Chelsea, her three-year-old daughter, learning how to live within a budget. She'd made several new acquaintances, but no other truly close friends yet. As for her love life—well, that was practically nonexistent. The few dates she'd accepted had been disappointing, to say the least. Too many men thought she was in dire need of their services in bed, and didn't react very graciously when she firmly informed them that they were mistaken. And too many men had no intention of being responsible for another man's child.

Maybe that explained why she was finding this wrong-number telephone call so entertaining. She really *was* hard up for adult companionship. Maybe she should get up her nerve to accept another one of the dinner invitations she'd been receiving lately. They couldn't *all* be toads, could they?

"You know, you should try to call your brother. He'd probably like to hear from you, especially if you're feeling a bit down."

Rather than taking offense at the unwarranted advice, Erin smiled again. "I would if I knew where he was," she replied. "As I said, he travels a lot. He's somewhere in Central America right now, I think. He'll call me as soon as he gets back into this country."

"Oh. Well, I guess I'd better call Cheryl. Again, I'm sorry about disturbing you with the call."

"Thank you. But don't apologize. Actually, I rather enjoyed it," she admitted.

"Oddly enough, so did I." He paused as the phone line crackled one last, faint time, then said, "Well, goodbye."

"Take care of that cold," she couldn't resist advising him, slipping back into her pseudo-maternal voice. After all, he was *someone's* brother.

"Thanks. I will. Bye, again."

"Goodbye." Feeling strangely reluctant, she hung up. She wondered if she'd only imagined that he'd seemed disinclined, as well, to sever their accidental connection.

She had just gotten up from the side of the bed when the phone rang again. Who could it be this time?

"You know, I just thought of something," that now familiar, cold-roughened voice said.

She smiled. "What?"

"Your brother's still dating that terrible person you don't like."

Erin groaned. "Oh, dear, you're right. I hadn't even thought of that."

"Oh, well, keep working on him. Maybe you'll get to have your I-told-you-so speech yet. *My* sister's going to thoroughly enjoy hers."

Erin was laughing when he hung up as abruptly as he'd started speaking. She was still smiling when she tiptoed into Chelsea's room to make sure the storm hadn't disturbed her.

BRETT TRIED to concentrate on his work, but his thoughts kept wandering—wandering to the telephone on one corner of the desk that sat only a few feet from his drawing table. Frowning, he set pencil to paper one more time, then sighed and gave up. He wasn't in a creative mood that evening. He was fighting a strong, totally inappropriate urge to place a telephone call. A call to someone he'd never met, whose name he didn't know, but whose voice had haunted him for almost a week.

Impulsive by nature, Brett finally gave in to that urge and picked up the phone and dialed: 555-2029. He hadn't written the number down, but he hadn't forgotten it, either. If a man answered, he could always hang up, he reasoned with a wry grin at his rather juvenile thought processes.

"Hello?"

It wasn't a man. Definitely not a man. He tried to picture a face to go with that voice. He'd be willing to bet his brand-new T square that she was attractive. "I don't suppose you'd believe I dialed a wrong number again?"

She paused for only a moment. "If you did, we need to have a little lesson."

He relaxed. She didn't sound annoyed by his call. In fact, she sounded rather pleased. "What kind of lesson?"

"The difference between a six and a nine. A six has a little circle at the bottom, a nine has a little circle at the top. Your sister's number ends with the one with the circle at the bottom."

Grinning, Brett leaned back in the leather chair and crossed his argyle-covered feet on the desk in front of him. "I'll keep that in mind."

"Your voice sounds much better. Cold gone?"

"Yes, finally. I'm feeling a lot better now."

"That's nice. Um—" She paused delicately, then asked the question that had obviously been puzzling her ever since she'd realized who he was. "Why did you call?"

He thought about that a moment. Why *had* he called? "I don't know," he admitted at last. "I just wanted to talk to you again. I enjoyed our conversation last week. Besides," he added on a rush of inspiration, "you said you were a bit lonely. I was—um—worried about you."

The silence that followed expressed her surprise. "Why, that's very . . . thoughtful of you," she said at length. "But I'm fine, really. I have friends."

"I'm sure you have many friends," Brett replied quickly. So much for that excuse. He tried another. "Did you ever hear from your brother?"

"No, not yet." Her concern was evident in her voice. If he knew the guy, he'd go punch him out. Didn't the jerk know that his sister worried about him? Knowing his own sister, Cheryl, and her maternal instincts toward him, Brett could just imagine how this woman must feel at being so out of touch with her brother.

"You know," he said, rubbing the slight bump on the bridge of his once-broken nose in what was a habitual gesture, "the nice thing about talking to a stranger on the phone, long-distance, is that you don't have to worry about what you say, because you probably won't ever meet me. You don't even know my name. So, if you feel like talking, now's your chance. I have a feeling I'd even enjoy that weird sense of humor you say no one understands except Adam and Corey."

"Do you remember *every*thing I said last week?" she demanded with a startled laugh.

He did, actually. How could he have forgotten when he'd displayed an inexplicable tendency to replay the impromptu conversation over and over in his mind? "Most of it," he prevaricated, not wanting her to think he was some sort of nut case. "Tell me something you'd tell Adam if you were talking to him. Something you find funny," he added, curious about that sense of humor.

"Mmm," she murmured consideringly, and he realized in pleasure that she wasn't going to tell him to buzz off and hang up in his ear, which he'd half expected her to do. "Well," she began, "I had a call from my ex-husband's ex-wife today. I laughed myself silly when it was over, but some people may have questioned my sanity for doing so. Adam would've understood."

"Your ex-husband's ex-wife?" Brett repeated slowly, enjoying the conversation immensely.

"Yep. She was his first wife. She's forty now and still moping about being divorced by him six years ago. Now she wants me to join her in forming a 'support club' of former wives who were dumped for younger, prettier women. Can you believe that?"

"How old are you?" he asked, emboldened by anonymity.

"Twenty-six."

He blinked. "A forty-year-old woman wants someone who's only twenty-six to help her start a club for dumped wives? Does she think you're going to spend the rest of your life sulking because your marriage ended in disappointment?"

"That's exactly what she thinks. After all, it's what she's doing."

"Um, you weren't the 'younger, prettier' woman he left *her* for, were you?" he mocked, knowing she could always hang up if he insulted her.

"No, thank God. I met him a year after his divorce. He'd already been through a couple of younger women before me. I was twenty-one, he had just turned forty and was positively terrified of growing older—though I didn't realize it at the time. I noticed that he liked to show me off to his friends, but I thought it was because he really cared about me. I got the old story about how his first wife didn't understand him—and I fell for it, hook, line and sinker. I was one of the few of my friends who wasn't married at the time. I guess I was ready to be swept off my feet."

"Smooth talker, was he?"

"The smoothest. We were married six weeks after we met. On our honeymoon I suspected I'd made a mistake. Within a few months, I *knew* I had. And then, just after his forty-first birthday, he told me that I was cramping his style. He bought a Porsche sports car and a couple of gold chains, and let his hair grow enough to make a little ponytail at his nape. He's spent the four years since our divorce making an utter ass of himself. Poor schlemiel thinks he's living the true playboy life-style. I don't think anyone's had the heart to tell him that even Hef finally got tired of that and settled down."

"I know that guy!" Brett exclaimed, keeping his tone light. "Actually, I know several just like him. They think young women keep *them* young. I've always thought the young women just made them look old in comparison. Besides, what can you talk about with a woman who was born after the Beatles made their debut on Ed Sullivan's show?"

"*I* was born after the Beatles were on Ed Sullivan's show," she reminded him.

Brett winced and ran a hand through his curly brown hair. "Yeah, you were, weren't you? Oh, well, if it makes you feel any better, I don't remember that year very clearly myself."

"How old are you?"

"Thirty-four."

"Married?" The question was asked just a bit too casually.

"No," he told her. "I have to admit I haven't been in any hurry to tie myself down to a commitment like that. But I'm *not* another woman-user like your ex-husband, believe me."

"The woman who wasn't as pretty on the inside as on the outside—did you think about marrying her?"

He grimaced when he thought of Sheree. "No," he confessed. "But—"

"She was gorgeous," the woman said flatly. "She looked good at your side, knew a few interesting tricks in bed, kept your blood pumping for a while. I know the story. It's the one my husband gave me about the woman he dumped me for."

Brett whistled softly. "Wow! He *did* work you over, didn't he?"

"I'm not as bitter as that sounded. I know not all men are like Martin. I'm just still annoyed with myself for being so gullible." She sighed loudly.

"You were very young."

"And very naive. Thank goodness I've gotten beyond that stage now."

Brett smiled. "All grown up now?"

"You betcha."

Chuckling, he wished again that he knew what she looked like. Obviously she was attractive, or the idiot she'd married wouldn't have been interested in her in the first place. Somehow he'd known all along that she was someone a man would notice. After all, she'd captured *his* attention—and he hadn't even laid eyes on her. "You wouldn't fall for a smooth-talking Romeo now?"

"No way."

"Not even if he looked like Tom Cruise or Mel Gibson?" he teased.

"We-e-l-l . . ." She drawled the word deliberately, making him laugh.

"Typical," he goaded her. "Show a woman a handsome face and she forgets all her lofty pronouncements on wisdom and caution."

"Oh, and men are better?" she immediately countered. "You've just come out of a bad relationship, yourself, but I'd bet you'd walk through fire for a chance at meeting Kim Basinger."

"Actually, I prefer petite blond starlets," he teased.

"Ah. The protective type, are you?"

"Let's just say I've got normally active hormones. How are yours?"

After only the slightest pause, she replied a bit faintly, "How are my whats?"

"Your hormones. You've been divorced four years, you said. You surely haven't sworn off men altogether."

"There hasn't been anyone since the divorce," she admitted. "Mostly because I've been too busy getting back on my feet to even contemplate getting involved with anyone. I started seeing someone a year ago, but it didn't work out. Actually, it was a disaster. But that doesn't mean I've given up on men. They have their uses," she added tauntingly, obviously enjoying their sparring as much as he.

"You're talking about affairs," he suggested.

"That's right," she agreed equably. "A series of discreet, careful affairs, entered with open eyes, closed heart and a pocketful of protection against pregnancy and disease. And thank heavens I'm never going to see you," she added in the same breath, "because I *never* talk like this to people I know!"

Brett laughed, believing her. He attempted to ignore the discomfort her words roused in him. Why should he suspect that this woman would be terribly disappointed in the life-style she'd just described? He thought of a tender young heart torn by her husband's callousness. Wounds like that were healed with love and tenderness—not breezy, no-strings affairs. Would she listen if he tried to tell her that?

No. She wouldn't. Not from a stranger over the phone. He only hoped for her sake that some nice guy would come along and convince her that love didn't have to hurt; didn't always lead to heartache. "It's kind of fun to talk to a stranger, isn't it? Not to have to guard your words or worry about what the other person thinks of you," he mused.

"You know, it *is* fun," she said, laughing. "Maybe we've stumbled onto something here—the reason all those 900 numbers are making a fortune. Dial a stranger and pour out your secret thoughts. 'Telephone therapy.' What do you think?"

He chuckled. "I think you're right. Only *I* called you, remember?"

"Oops. I don't think you're going to make very much at this if you're the one footing the bill. Don't you have any deep-hidden anger you want to get out of your system while you've got me on the line? Just to make the call worth your money?"

Pleased at the smile he detected in her voice, he shook his head, forgetting for the moment that she couldn't see him. "I think it was worth my money, anyway. It's been very interesting."

"Better than TV, right?"

"Right."

"By the way, did your sister enjoy her I-told-you-so speech, or did you get out of it because you were sick?"

The memory made him cringe. "I wish. She went on for a good ten minutes about my lack of judgment and told me she wished I'd let her pick out a good woman for me."

"So, why don't you?" she teased.

"The last woman my sister introduced me to had dollar signs in her eyes and fangs behind her sweetly smiling lips," Brett replied bluntly. "The one before that had the IQ and conversational ability of a doorknob. The one before *that*—"

"Okay, I get the picture." She was laughing. "My brother has similar complaints about the women I've tried to fix him up with."

"What about him? Did he like Martin?" Brett couldn't resist asking.

"Hated him," she said with a sigh. "Too bad *I* didn't listen when he was the one giving advice."

"Did he say 'I told you so'?"

Her voice noticeably softened. "No, he didn't, though he certainly could have. He was wonderful. Still is."

When you hear from him, Brett thought, but kept it to himself. "Must be that brothers are more noble than sisters. We don't feel the need to rub your noses in it when we're right."

"Yeah, sure. If you only knew how many times he *has* gloated about being right when I was wrong . . ."

Remembering a few of those times between himself and his own sister, Brett refrained from comment. "It's getting late." It was already past eleven in Boston, though he knew it was an hour earlier in Arkansas. At last he knew now that there was no man impatiently waiting in bed for her. "Guess I'd better let you go."

"I suppose you'd better," she agreed quietly.

"I hope you hear from Adam soon."

"I will. He always keeps in touch when he can. It's just—difficult for him, with the way he travels."

"You know, I could give you my number. If you ever need to talk again—"

"I don't think so," she interrupted gently. "But thanks for the offer."

"Yeah. Well, goodbye. Be happy, okay?"

"You, too."

"Thanks. Bye."

"Bye."

Had her voice really sounded rather wistful when they'd said goodbye? Or was he only projecting his own feelings onto her? Why on earth should he find himself sorry that the conversation had ended, knowing he'd probably never talk to her again? They lived half a continent away from each other, for pete's sake, and she had indicated that she had no interest in pursuing any further acquaintance with him. Nor, if he was honest, was he all that interested in actually meeting her, beyond curiosity.

Fresh out of a disastrous relationship, he was in no hurry to enter another one—particularly with someone who'd been burned as badly as whatever-her-name-was. It was going to require someone very special to take away her scars; someone patient, selfless, infinitely loving. Someone extraordinary. *He* was about as ordinary as they came, Brett admitted matter-of-factly, catching a glimpse of his not-very-tall, not-terribly-handsome, brown-haired, brown-eyed reflection in the mirror on the opposite wall of his office. His sister accused him of staying young looking just to make her feel older. More than once he'd regretted the dimples and curls that, combined with his lack of impressive height, kept him from being a "major hunk," in the words of his best friend's teenage daughter. And the woman on the phone must be beautiful, judging by the tastes of the unpleasant Martin.

He really had to stop wondering about her. He didn't know her, had never seen her, would never meet her. Sure, she sounded nice, but he was notorious for being a sucker for a husky voice and feminine laughter. How many times had he been roped in by them only to find himself with a man-eating barracuda on his hands?

Get back to work, Nash. You're on a deadline, remember?

Trying to put her out of his mind, he sat in front of the drawing board again, reaching for his charcoal pencil. His creative mind was weaving stories again, and he needed to confine himself to the comic books he wrote and illustrated. The kind that made money. Mistaking fantasy for reality could lead to nothing more than disappointment.

ERIN SAT BY HER PHONE for several long minutes after the call ended, feeling like an idiot for telling her entire life's story to a stranger on the telephone. *What must he be thinking of someone with so little discretion?* she wondered with a low moan.

Then, after thinking about it for a few uncomfortable minutes, she decided that he really had seemed to enjoy talking to her, and to sympathize with her story of her failed marriage—something she rarely discussed these days. When *was* the last time she'd expressed her feelings so honestly?

Sure, she talked to Adam when she had the chance, but even with him she wasn't completely open, so that he wouldn't worry too much about her when he was away and had to concentrate on his own problems. Adam's job was a dangerous one—more dangerous, she suspected, than he wanted her to know—and he needed to focus all his attention on staying in one piece.

Corey was secluded in the mountains, and Chelsea was only three, so no wonder she'd done everything but open a vein when her mystery caller had offered an ear. All those words had been building up for a long time.

He was the one who'd made the call. He'd gotten what he'd asked for. And she felt much better for it. *So why feel badly?*

He'd never call again, of course. Why should he? They were total strangers. This second call had probably been an impulse just to satisfy his curiosity about the woman he'd accidentally talked to a week earlier.

He'd sounded so nice, she thought as she moved quietly through the house turning off lights, careful not to disturb her sleeping daughter. But then, lots of men sounded nice—and weren't, once you got to know them. Perhaps talking so frankly to a stranger on the telephone wasn't the brightest thing she'd ever done. Adam would probably have a fit if he ever found out. He was so over-protective of his only sister. It was because of him that her number wasn't listed in the telephone directory.

She'd be more careful from now on. No more chatty calls with strangers, no matter how safe the anonymous conversation might seem. She wasn't a silly girl any longer, but a mature, responsible mother who'd carved herself a secure, if sometimes just a tiny bit dull, niche. She was Chelsea's mom, and perfectly content with that role.

Climbing into her empty bed, she told herself that she really didn't mind sleeping alone. It was safer that way.

Lonely, perhaps. But safe.

Why didn't she find more comfort in that reassurance?

2

ERIN TURNED OFF the television with a sigh. *What garbage!* She was annoyed with herself for watching the badly written disease-of-the-week movie. But Chelsea was asleep, she had nothing new to read, and housework certainly wasn't something she did for entertainment. What else was there to do? She'd finished all her free-lance art assignments for Redding & Howard, the advertising agency that was her steadiest client. There was nothing else pending at the moment.

She was bored.

She stretched, then glanced at her watch. Nine-thirty. Maybe she'd just go to bed.

The phone rang.

It couldn't be, she told herself even as her heart jumped. It had been two weeks since she'd heard from Mr. Wrong Number. She was certain he'd forgotten all about her. More likely it was Adam. He'd called her as soon as he'd gotten back into the country the week before. He'd missed her, and was frustrated that he couldn't get away from work for time with Erin and Chelsea.

It had been wonderful talking to him, but oddly enough she'd thought of her mystery caller all during her long conversation with Adam. *Must be guilt,* she rationalized, determined not to let her brother know that she'd participated in anything so imprudent. "Hello."

"Hi."

Funny that she recognized the voice. Even after two weeks. Even with only that one syllable. Helpless to restrain it, she felt a smile tilt the corners of her mouth. "Hi, yourself. Did you get the little circles on your numbers mixed up again?"

"I've got this terrible problem with curiosity. My sister's always said it was a good thing I wasn't born a cat."

"What are you curious about this time?" she asked, amused at his sheepish tone.

"Did you ever hear from your brother?"

"Yes, I did. He's back in California—for a while, anyway."

"What does he do?"

"He works for the government."

"Out of California?"

"That's right. He doesn't like D.C.," she explained as if that made perfect sense.

"Oh." He paused, then asked with studied nonchalance, "How are you? Everything going okay?"

"Yes, fine." She paused, unsure how to continue. Wondering why he'd called again. Wishing she weren't quite so glad that he had. "Um—how's Cheryl?"

He chuckled at the question. "She's fine. And Adam?"

"He said he was okay. Not that he'd tell me if he wasn't," she added candidly. "He's a bit overprotective when it comes to me."

He didn't respond. Instead he asked, "Heard any more from your ex-husband's ex-wife?"

"Yes, as a matter of fact, I did. I told her I had better things to do than sit around with a group of women whining about the men who'd done them wrong."

"Good for you!" he approved with a quick laugh.

Reveling in the compliment, she tossed her head, which made her dark hair fly out before settling in a sleek curtain around her shoulders. "She was highly indignant. Told me I didn't even have enough sense to know that I needed the support of other poor unfortunates."

"That's got to be one depressing woman."

"She'd be okay if she'd forget about Martin and get on with her life," Erin replied. "Which is exactly what I told her. I suggested that she go out and have a teeth-rattling affair. It would do her a world of good."

"This from a woman who hasn't—um—*been* with anyone since her divorce?"

She shrugged, hoping the gesture carried in her voice when she answered. "Haven't you ever heard the old saying, 'Do as I say, not as I do'?"

She heard a shuffling sound and a muffled squeak. She pictured him leaning back in a deep leather chair, then wondered what he looked like. She knew his age, but nothing else. Was he blond? Dark? Red-haired? Tall? Short? Lean? Fat? He didn't sound fat, she thought, smiling at her own foolishness.

"I suppose after four years of celibacy, you must be getting a bit . . . itchy," he said boldly.

Her cheeks heated and she was grateful he couldn't see her. He really did seem to remember every word she'd said to him. "Well . . . sometimes," she admitted.

He paused, seemingly intrigued by her tone. She could almost see him cocking his head in curiosity, though she still didn't know what color hair topped that head—if any at all. "Martin wasn't such a great lover?" he hazarded. "Not surprising," he went on before she had to respond. "The man you described would be much more interested in his own pleasure than his partner's."

"Unlike you, I suppose?" she taunted, amazed at her daring. What was it that got into her when she talked to this man?

"Are you asking if I'm any good in bed?" he challenged, sounding amused.

"I suppose I am," she acknowledged rather dazedly.

"Hmm . . ."

He drew the monosyllable out, as if giving the matter a great deal of thought. "It's hard to rate one's own performance, of course. But I haven't had many complaints."

"Many?" she repeated, fighting the urge to giggle.

"Well, there was one girl, back when I was a novice. She—um—she'd been around a bit, I guess you could say. I think I was a bit clumsy. Perhaps a little too . . . precipitate."

"And have you had a great deal of practice since that unsuccessful effort?"

"I'm not into one-night stands, if that's what you're asking. Even if I were, that sort of behavior is too dangerous, these days. Let's just say that I'm no longer a novice."

Erin sighed. "It's so different for men."

"In what way?"

"You can admit to having experience and it's considered admirable. A woman still has to worry about her reputation, about being thought easy—all that double-standard garbage."

"Oh, I don't think it's quite that bad anymore. Surely not."

"Oh, really?" she asked skeptically. "What would you say if I said I'd been with dozens of men?"

"Well, for starters, I'd wonder where you'd found the time in only twenty-six years. Then I'd point out that *anyone*, man or woman, who'd been with dozens of lovers is somewhat less than discriminating. I don't think you've had a great deal of experience."

"How do you know that?" she questioned.

"Call it a hunch. Am I right?"

She sighed heavily. "You're right. Martin was the first."

"Oh. I'm really sorry to hear that.'

This time she couldn't hold back a giggle. This man had the most incredible ability to make her feel better—about lots of things. "Believe me, I am, too. I haven't had a lot of luck with romance, actually. Something always goes wrong, someone always ends up being hurt. It's very difficult, isn't it?"

"If you want to fly to Boston, I'd be happy to volunteer my services in one area, at least," he offered humorously.

Hearing the teasing behind his words, Erin laughed. "I think not. I like our relationship exactly the way it is."

"But we don't even know each other's name."

"Right. There's a kind of freedom in that, don't you think? It's like—like having a pen pal without going to all the trouble of composing a letter."

"Telephone pen pals? Interesting concept."

"It is, isn't it? Of course, it's a bit more expensive than a postage stamp. You're going to have a hefty phone bill this month."

"That's okay. I make a hefty salary," he admitted airily.

That didn't surprise her. Somehow she'd sensed that he was successful at whatever it was he did. She didn't ask for specifics. As she'd said, she rather liked keeping him a fantasy man. It was fun, intellectually stimulating—and safe. Even if he knew her name, it would be unlikely that he could find her—if he were someone to worry about; and her instincts told her that he could be trusted.

"Does that mean it's okay if I call you again sometime—just to talk?" he asked a bit too casually, making her suspect that he really wanted her to agree.

"You don't think this is a little . . . strange?"

He didn't even hesitate. "No. You're the one who compared it to pen pals. There's not a lot of difference, is there?"

She was terribly tempted. It really was nice to have this new friend to talk to; someone with whom she didn't have to pretend, didn't have to guard what she said—almost like a child's imaginary friend. What harm could there be in it? "Sure, you can call again sometime."

"And will you do me a favor?"

"What?" she asked warily.

"Write down my number. You don't have to know my name, if you really want to keep it that way, but I'd like to know you have my number if you ever need to talk. Will you do that?"

She couldn't imagine ever having the nerve to pick up the phone and call him, but she sensed the genuine concern in his deep voice. "All right."

She could hear his smile when he recited the number, which she dutifully wrote down in the back of her telephone directory. No name beside it. She'd know whose number it was. "I have it."

"Good. So I'll talk to you again sometime."

"All right."

"Good night."

"Good night." Bemused, she hung up the phone. And then she started to laugh.

"WHAT'S YOUR FAVORITE food?" he asked, when he called again.

This was their fifth conversation in the six weeks since he first called her by accident. "Any kind of seafood—especially crab."

"What's your favorite movie?"

Erin thought about it a moment. There were lots of movies she liked, but her favorite? "Either *Somewhere in Time* or *Same Time, Next Year*," she decided.

"Ah. A romantic," he teased. "And a bit of a maverick—not particularly interested in the critics' opinions."

"There was nothing wrong with either of those movies," she replied defensively. "They were both well written, well acted, and they touched my emotions. I always cry when Richard goes back to his own time in *Somewhere in Time*—the scene where he breaks down and cries. And when Alan Alda cries over the death of his—or rather, George's—son in *Same Time, Next Year*, it always gets to me, no matter how many times I've seen it."

"Oh, so you like seeing men cry."

She chuckled. "Poetic justice. Think of how many tears women have shed over men."

"You think men don't cry over women?"

"Have you ever?" she asked, curious and knowing he'd answer honestly. They'd both taken advantage of their odd circumstances to talk quite candidly. Better than therapy, they'd agreed.

"Yeah. As a matter of fact, I have."

She stretched comfortably on her stomach on the couch, propped on her elbows as she pressed the phone to her ear. "Tell me about it."

"My first serious relationship was when I was a senior in college. She dumped me because I was too short. And— I confess—I cried that night. I was really hung up on her and that seemed like such a stupid reason to break up."

"You're right, it does. Why would she dump you because you're too short? Didn't she notice how tall you were when you started dating?"

"Yeah, but she thought I was cute," he answered glumly. "Then I guess her girlfriends started teasing her—she was four inches taller than me. When she was elected home-coming queen, she started thinking about how it would look when I escorted her onto the platform. So she dumped me for a six-five basketball player."

"What a bimbo," Erin pronounced scornfully.

He laughed. "Yeah, I think she was. But she was gorgeous."

Her sigh adequately expressed her disgust. "This society is entirely too hung up on personal appearance. I mean, you've been hurt because you're not a six-footer. I was married because Martin thought I looked good beside him, which led to disaster. Appearance makes a difference in political races, hiring practices, social success. It's ridiculous. What we need is less emphasis on appearance, and more on character."

"A meeting of minds," he suggested.

"Exactly."

"Like we have."

That took her aback for a moment. "Well . . . yes, I suppose so."

"No, really. We've become friends without even seeing each other, just because we enjoy talking and have some things in common. I really like you . . . and I have no idea what you look like."

"None?" she teased.

"Well . . ."

Her feet kicked faster in enjoyment. "Tell me what you think I look like."

"You're pretty."

She all but snarled. "We've already established that—it's one of my problems, remember? Besides, 'pretty' is in the eye of the beholder. *I* don't think I'm all that special, but some men seem to think so. And didn't we just agree that had nothing to do with it?"

"Oh, it doesn't," he assured her. "I'd enjoy talking to you even if you bore a strong resemblance to George C. Scott. But you asked what I picture when I think of you. And I think you're pretty."

"I want details."

He chuckled. "Okay. Your hair is either auburn or brunette."

She twirled a near-black strand around her finger. "Right."

"Which?"

"One of the two. What else?"

He sighed but continued. "Eyes either green or blue."

"Very good."

"One of the guesses is right?" he asked dryly.

"Yep. Anything else?"

"I have this sneaky suspicion you're tall," he said heavily.

She swallowed a giggle. "I guess that depends on whether I'm being compared to Dudley Moore or Magic Johnson."

"So how *do* you feel about Dudley Moore?" he asked hopefully.

"I think he's cute."

"Yeah. Somehow I thought you'd say that." He sounded thoroughly disgusted.

"See? You've got me down pat."

"Oh, sure. You're either auburn or dark-haired, blue- or green-eyed, and you're somewhere between Dudley and Magic in height. Perfect description. Any detective should be able to walk right up to you."

"Mmm." She tried to picture him. "I think your hair is brown."

"What shade?"

"Light—or medium. Your eyes, too."

"What about them?"

"Brown."

"Could be."

"Hey, I told you when your guesses were right."

"Yeah, but I gave you more choices. What else?"

"You're not very tall."

He snorted. "Gee, how did you ever figure *that* out?"

Ignoring him, she continued, "You have a nice smile. Probably dimples."

"You think so?" He sounded startled. She grinned, guessing that she was right on target with the dimples. "Why?"

"You just sound so cute," she crooned.

For the first time in five conversations, she heard him use an obscenity.

"*Cute* is not a favorite word?" she hazarded through a giggle.

"*Not* a favorite word," he confirmed. "Can't we talk about something else?"

"What's your favorite food?" she asked, mimicking his earlier cross-examination.

"Boston scrod. What else?"

"You know, there are times when you don't sound like a Bostonian. You sound like someone from around here, almost. Are you?"

"Close. I grew up in Memphis. I've been here long enough that my sister accuses me of sounding like a Yankee, but every time I visit her, I find myself talking Southern again. Guess I'm one of those who picks up the accents of people around me."

"Mmm. So that's how your sister ended up in North Little Rock?"

"Yeah. Married a guy from there. I came east to college and ended up staying."

"Harvard?"

"Yup. What else do you want to know about me?"

Wow. Harvard! "Are your parents still living?"

"Yes. They moved to Florida a few years ago. I see them a couple of times a year."

"Uh—do you like children?" Erin frowned as soon as the question left her mouth. She hadn't even realized she was going to ask that one. Why *had* she? she wondered, her gaze turning toward Chelsea's bedroom door.

"Sure, I like kids," he answered breezily. "From a distance." And then he laughed.

Damn. Another one. Some men just didn't like children, didn't want the responsibility. Martin certainly hadn't. Her own father had resented being tied down to a wife and two children; finally he'd walked out—when Erin was just a baby. Adam seemed to enjoy Chelsea, but admitted he was in no hurry to have any children himself, if ever. And then there'd been Scott, a man she'd dated briefly last year. She'd found out exactly how he felt about children in a most unpleasant way.

And now she'd discovered that her friend was another one. If she'd had any hope that anything could ever develop between them, it died then. She wouldn't risk another disaster like the one that had almost occurred with Scott.

"Hey—you still awake? No more questions?"

Erin forced herself to speak lightly. After all, this was still her telephone friend. No more than an enjoyable fantasy. Nothing had changed, right? "Okay, favorite movie."

"Almost any animated Disney film."

Erin blinked and pulled the receiver away to stare at it for a moment. Then she brought it back to her ear. *"Disney?"* she repeated carefully, wondering if she'd understood.

"Yeah. Their animation is incredible, isn't it? I mean, there have been a few clunkers, but on the whole, the stuff's great. Have you seen *The Little Mermaid?* Wonderfully done."

She'd rented the movie only a few weeks before, actually, and watched it with Chelsea. She didn't mention that fact because she hadn't mentioned Chelsea at all, telling herself it was for safety reasons. "I agree that the animation is wonderful, but surely you don't think it's better than *Fantasia.*"

"Oh, well, of course *Fantasia* is amazing—the ultimate in animation. But I prefer *The Little Mermaid*, because, not only is it beautifully done, but it has a strong story that holds the interest of children *and* adults. That's the real test."

"How about some of the other animated features—non-Disney work?"

"Puh-leeze."

She laughed, and named two of the more impressive animated features of the past few years—*The Secret of NIMH* and *An American Tail.*

"Hey, you really know about this stuff, don't you?"

She glanced at the open door of the spare bedroom that served as her office, the one next to the room in which Chelsea was sleeping. Her drawing board was just visible in the shadows. "Let's just say I'm very interested in art."

"Really? Me, too. In fact, I sort of work in the field."

"So do I."

"Yeah? What do you do?"

But that was getting too specific. She couldn't keep him in her fantasies if he started to get too real. "Art stuff," she answered vaguely.

"Oh." He sounded a bit disgruntled at her reticence, but he didn't protest. "Well, still, it's pretty interesting that we have this in common. If we ever actually meet, we'll compare work. What do you say?"

Her throat tightened. "Uh—meet? You mean—in person?"

"Well, yeah. Maybe sometime when I'm in Arkansas visiting my sister, we could get together for a drink or something. I don't have any plans to visit there now, but sometime, maybe—"

"Mommy!"

The sleepy, bad-dream cry brought Erin upright on the couch. "I've got to go."

"Was it something I said?" he asked, startled.

"No, of course not. It's just that—there's something I have to do," she explained hastily, as Chelsea cried out again. "Goodbye."

"Bye."

She'd hung up before he had the syllable out. Reality had intruded into fantasy.

BRETT WAS FROWNING when he hung up the phone. What had happened to make her hang up so abruptly? They'd been having a perfectly pleasant conversation. Had it bothered her that he'd even hinted they might meet at some point? If so, she was carrying this secrecy thing a bit too far. They'd become friends, in a way, and he was in North Little Rock every few years to see his sister. Why shouldn't he and...and— Hell, he wished he at least knew her name. Anyway, why shouldn't they get together sometime? Just a drink, maybe. Dinner, perhaps.

If anything else developed—well, what would be wrong with that?

Shaking his head, he shoved the phone across the desk and stood, telling himself that maybe he wouldn't call her again for a while. He needed a real flesh-and-blood woman in his life, not just a sexy voice on a phone line.

It *was* time for a visit with his sister. Deciding to do just that, he sauntered out of his office in search of a late-night snack.

BRETT'S RESOLVE lasted less than a week. He'd been working on a comic book for too long when he became aware of a peculiar sensation that the telephone on his desk was growing larger and larger the more he ignored it. Had he drawn that particular scene in a comic, he'd have had the phone sneaking a bit closer to the man's elbow when he looked away, only to stop dead in its tracks each time the man turned to check. He might even have sketched in a broken-line balloon above the instrument containing tiny letters spelling out, "Call her."

Sighing with disgust, he swiveled on his stool, glared at his phone and growled, "Shut up!"

Brett checked his watch. Ten in the evening. Just about the time he usually called her. Well, hell . . .

He picked up the receiver and punched out the digits he'd memorized.

"Hello?"

Funny how familiar her voice had become. Like that of a close friend. Or a woman with whom he was rapidly becoming obsessed.

"Hi. It's me."

"Oh, hi. How are you?"

He settled more comfortably in the chair for another long conversation with the woman whose name he didn't even know. "I'm losing my sanity."

"Oh? How can you tell?" she teased.

He grinned. Now he remembered why he kept calling her. She made him laugh. "Are you implying that I'm a bit shaky at the best of times?"

"Well, you have to understand that I haven't seen you under exactly normal circumstances."

"You haven't seen me at all," he pointed out.

"True. Why are you suddenly questioning your sanity?"

"I've been talking to my phone."

"That's what phones are for."

"Yeah, but there wasn't anyone at the other end of the line."

She paused for only a moment. "We may have a problem here."

He chuckled. "Didn't I say so? I think celibacy is dulling the old gray matter."

"So, who's been making you remain celibate?"

"I have, I guess," he answered after a moment's thought. "I've never been interested in sleeping with strangers and I don't particularly want to go to bed with anyone I know at the moment."

"Hmm. That *is* a problem. What are you going to do about it?"

"I'm considering flying to North Little Rock and seducing *you*," he murmured outrageously, just to test her reaction. "What do you think?"

"I think you were right earlier. You *are* losing your sanity," she informed him sternly, though she sounded more amused than insulted. That was another thing he liked about her. She knew how to take a joke.

Or had it been a joke?

Deciding not to dwell on that particular question, he carried the subject further. "Well, just in case I ever *do* try to seduce you, how should I go about it? I used to be a Boy Scout," he added, "and I like to be prepared."

"I'm not quite sure I understand the question. What do you mean, how would you seduce me? I assume you've conducted a few seductions in the past. A seduction's a seduction, isn't it?"

Brett pulled the receiver away from his ear and stared at it as if he were studying her face. Was she really that naive? "Boy," he said when he brought the phone back into place, "Martin really *was* a lousy lover, wasn't he?"

She murmured something he didn't quite catch and didn't ask her to repeat.

"A seduction," he went on meaningfully, "is *not* just a seduction. It's different for everyone. What turns one woman on may turn you completely off."

"I suppose that's true. I don't think I'd care much for leather and chains and whips."

Laughing, he raised one hand to massage the back of his neck, trying to ignore that his body was beginning to react to the suggestive conversation. It was all too easy to imagine himself seducing this particular woman—and he'd never even seen her, he reminded himself, rather dazed. "No? So what would turn you on?" he asked, trying to believe he was only teasing and not making notes for future reference.

"I can't believe we're having this conversation."

"Call it a fantasy. What would be your idea of the ultimate seduction?"

She hesitated for so long that he was beginning to think she wouldn't answer. He didn't for the life of him know why he wanted so much for her to do so.

"I guess I'm pretty traditional," she said at last, rather shyly. "Flowers, soft music, a crackling fire."

He'd half expected that from this woman. He already knew she was quite traditional in some ways. Delightful ways. "A bearskin rug?"

"Oh, no. I wouldn't want to make love on some poor animal's hide."

He choked on a laugh. "Um—yeah, right. So you've described the setting. Now, what about the man? Tall, dark and handsome? Hulking blond lifeguard?" He grimaced as he asked the question.

"We've talked about this before, remember? I'm not particularly interested in appearances. He just has to be . . . special. Amusing, interesting, caring. Unselfish."

Brett wondered if she was aware that she'd just revealed a great deal about her relationship with her ex. "Would you like for me—er—*him* to whisper pretty words in your ear? Snippets of poetry, perhaps?"

"I'd feel really stupid if some guy started quoting poetry to me," she returned with a laugh. "'Shall I compare thee to a summer's day . . . ?' Too Hollywood."

"What about the pretty words?"

"That might be nice," she replied slowly, a bit wistfully. "But only if he meant them," she added almost in the same breath. "And I'd know if he didn't . . . if they were just part of an act."

"Okay. So we have flowers, music, a fire, and soft, heartfelt words. What else? What about the actual love-making? You like it slow and easy? Hot and rough? Do you lie back and enjoy or take the initiative yourself? Do you like to make love once and go to sleep or keep at it all night?" Grinning enormously, he waited for her to stop him.

Her moan of embarrassment was just what he'd expected. "Stop," she begged. "I can't deal with this."

"Turning you on, huh?" He squirmed restlessly in his chair, realizing uncomfortably that the words held true in reverse.

"No, that's enough," she ordered firmly. "Really."

"Okay," he conceded. "I didn't mean to embarrass you."

"Yes, you did."

He laughed. "You're right, I did. You're cute when you blush."

"I— How did you know I was blushing?"

"Your voice was blushing. It's getting late. Guess I'd better let you go."

"All right. I think I'll go splash cool water on my voice."

"Do that. Bye."

"Goodbye. Um—?"

"Yes?" he prompted.

"*All* night?" she asked delicately.

Remembering what he'd asked her about keeping at it all night, he laughed again. "It's been done."

"Have you ever—er—?"

"Now *I'm* blushing. Good night."

"Good night."

Brett hung up, groaned, and decided he'd take a shower before turning in. Maybe he'd make it a cold one. He knew he wouldn't get much sleep that night.

Erin didn't sleep particularly well, either. She found herself squirming restlessly against the pillows well into the night, for some reason. She had only to close her eyes to picture herself lying on a thick, handmade quilt before a crackling fire, with flowers and candles scenting the air, her nude, aching body being caressed by a man with skillful hands—a man who murmured soft, seductive words in Brett's deep, now familiar voice.

She groaned and swallowed convulsively. Fantasies were exciting, but certainly proved uncomfortable at times. Trying to block them from her mind, she buried her face in the pillow and ignored the urgings of long-suppressed needs. She couldn't imagine why they had suddenly resurfaced after so many months of self-denial.

3

"Is it done yet, Mommy? Can I have a bite?" Chelsea bounced eagerly at Erin's feet, her dark ponytail bobbing.

"No, darling. I haven't cooked them yet." Erin demonstrated that the square pan was filled with brownie mixture and ready to go into the oven. "It's not good to eat until it's been cooked."

Chelsea plopped into a chair at the kitchen table, her arms crossed resignedly over her chest. "Brownies take for*ever*," she proclaimed.

Erin closed the oven door. "I know. And they'll have to cool after I take them out," she warned. "They'll be too hot to eat at first."

Chelsea groaned loudly and hid her face behind chubby hands.

Chuckling at her three-year-old daughter's antics, Erin opened the refrigerator. "How about a glass of juice for now?"

"Okay. But don't forget the brownies," Chelsea warned.

Erin solemnly promised not to forget the brownies.

She'd just set the glass of juice on the table when the doorbell rang.

"I'll get it!" Chelsea cried, scrambling out of the chair and dashing for the door.

"No! Chelsea, don't open that door," Erin warned, hurrying after her. Though she was an exceptionally well-behaved and mature little girl, Chelsea's insatiable curiosity was the one trait that most often got her into trouble. Lately she'd taken to answering the door and the phone, though Erin was trying to teach her not to.

She was glad her Boston telephone friend always called at night, after Chelsea was in bed and wasn't likely to grab the phone. They'd been carrying on their lengthy, laughter-filled, sometimes astonishingly frank conversations for eight weeks and Erin still hadn't mentioned Chelsea, though there was little else her mystery friend didn't know about Erin by now. She'd told him things about herself that no one else on earth knew—embarrassing incidents, private fantasies, lost dreams, past disappointments.

In return, he'd done the same. She'd learned so much about him, and had been startled to discover that men's private thoughts weren't so very different from women's, once the restraints of face-to-face conversation were dispensed with, thanks to the anonymity provided by the phone. Martin had certainly never been so candid. Nor had Adam who, though he never failed to provide a sympathetic ear for Erin, had never been one to talk much about himself.

All that honesty was another reason Erin looked forward to talking to her new friend—and another reason she told herself she'd never want to actually meet him, no matter what fantasies were beginning to weave themselves into in her dreams. Dreams in which his now-so-familiar voice murmured pretty words into her eager ears while his hands stroked her love-starved body and he looked down at her with a melting smile bracketed by deep, endearing dimples.

Trying not to think of those fantasies now, she looked out the small window of her front door before opening it, only to feel her eyes widen and her pulse quicken with pleasure. "Adam!"

Her brother's arms closed around her as soon as the door shut behind him. "Hi, sis."

"Adam, it's so good to see you." She lifted her face for his kiss without loosening her stranglehold around his neck, her toes dangling above the floor. Half an inch short of six feet, her brother stood well above her own five feet seven inches.

His dark, lean face softened only marginally with the half-smile he gave her—almost a grin for her usually serious sibling. His dark eyes, narrowed by hours of squinting into sun and shadow, reflected her own smile back at her. "You don't look half bad, yourself."

Her smile vanished abruptly. "Oh, Adam, what have you done to yourself *now?*" she wailed, her hand going up to his temple. He'd worn his fine, straight brown hair longer than usual, brushed to one side to fall over the temple on which she concentrated. Others might not have noticed the thin red scar beneath that thick lock. He'd probably known Erin wouldn't miss it even as he'd made a halfhearted effort to hide it.

"Nothing serious. Don't worry about it." He pulled away from her to turn to Chelsea, who was dancing impatiently at their feet. "Hello, pumpkin."

"Hi, Uncle Adam!" Chelsea launched herself into a vertical leap that took her straight into his waiting arms. She planted a noisy, juicy kiss on his cheek, then giggled as she poked a finger into the cleft in his chin. "Did you bring me something?"

"Chelsea—"

"Of course I brought you something," Adam said, overriding Erin's disapproval. "I brought you both something." He slanted a look at Erin. "I know you weren't expecting me, but I can stay a couple of days if you—"

"You know very well I'd throw a tantrum if you *didn't* stay," she broke in. "You don't need to make a reservation with me."

"Mommy's making brownies but they've got to cook and then they'll have to cool and where's my present?" Chelsea asked without pausing for breath.

With a husky chuckle, Adam tweaked the upturned tip of his niece's nose. "In my suitcase. You can have it if you promise that I can share your brownies."

"Well, of *course* you can share my brownies," Chelsea informed him. "Don't be ridic'lous."

Erin laughed at the quizzical look Adam gave her. "She's been watching television," she explained.

Adam nodded as if that made sense. Gravely, he tucked Chelsea under his arm and reached for his bag, listening to her chatter as he dug out the gifts he'd brought with him.

"MARTIN STILL MAKING a jerk of himself?" Adam asked laconically, as he sprawled on the couch with a beer clasped in one hand. They were sitting in her living room after a large dinner, enjoying the quiet now that Chelsea was finally asleep. Chelsea hadn't wanted to go to bed that night, claiming that she wanted to play with Uncle Adam, but he'd tucked her in, promising he'd be there when she woke the next morning.

Erin grimaced. "I keep hoping he'll get tired of being the laughingstock of the entire city, but he just gets worse and worse. He'll be forty-five next week, you know, and he's acting like a wild teenager." She shook her head in self-disgust. "I wish I knew what I'd ever seen in him in the first place."

"I think it had something to do with broad shoulders, blue eyes and a movie-star profile," he grumbled. "At least those were a few things you mentioned at the time."

Recalling her recent telephone monologue about judging people by appearance, Erin groaned. "I know. God, I was such an idiot."

Adam shrugged. "We all make mistakes."

"*You* don't."

He looked faintly startled. "The hell I don't."

Erin cocked her head. "Well, if you do, you always recover from them easily enough. And I can't imagine you ever letting yourself be taken in by a pair of blue eyes or falling for someone who's only using you to impress her friends."

He shrugged again. "So some of us make different mistakes than others."

Intrigued, she started to ask for specifics, but he forestalled her questions by asking another of his own. "Is Martin keeping up with his child-support payments?"

"Oh, yes, the checks come on exactly the same day every month. His secretary is very efficient. I'm surprised he doesn't send her over for a biweekly visit with Chelsea."

"He still doesn't visit her?"

"He told me he wouldn't when we split up. He reminds me occasionally that he never wanted a child in the first place and he'd told me so from the beginning. He heavily implies that the pregnancy was all my fault, then acts so self-righteous for fulfilling his financial obligations to her, anyway. How I'd love to tell him just where he can put his monthly checks."

"I know you haven't wanted to take any money from him from the beginning, but don't let him stop paying," he said flatly. "It's the least he can do for you and Chelsea. Dammit, Erin, it's the man's duty to see that the child he fathered is well cared for."

"*I* could support her," Erin argued stubbornly.

"Not working free-lance, you can't," he returned without hesitation. "And since you won't take any money from me, either, giving up the child support would mean you'd have to go back to work full-time. Is that what you want to do? I agreed with your decision to put her in that half-day preschool program to let her meet and play with other children, but do you really want to be away from her every day, all day?"

Erin leaned her head back against her chair and sighed. "No. I don't want to put her in day care. It's just pride talking, I guess."

"Exactly. And since you haven't spent one red cent of Martin's money on yourself, and you're putting most of it in savings for Chelsea's future, your pride shouldn't be in the least bruised. Hell, if you were any more self-sufficient you'd be living on a desert island somewhere," he added in a growl.

"Oh, you're one to talk," she retorted, her head lifting at his tone. "The original lone wolf—or are you still involved with that she-wolf who answered your phone that time I called and proceeded to inform me that she didn't want *any* other women calling you? Remember? The one who refused to believe I was your sister?"

The one whose parting she'd celebrated when she'd thought she was talking to Adam during that wrong-number call two months earlier, only to discover that some other sister had cause to celebrate. Erin didn't mention that, of course, knowing better than to tell Adam about her mystery caller.

"She was gone the next day," Adam muttered, looking down into his beer can.

"I can't say I'm sorry."

He shrugged. "Neither can I. I thought she knew the score from the beginning. Turned out I was wrong. Like I said, we all make mistakes."

"So, are you seeing anyone new?"

He shook his head. "Haven't had time to do much socializing lately. How about you?"

She cleared her throat, suddenly sorry she'd asked her question. She and Adam had had this conversation more than once during the past year and she already knew he disapproved of her reclusiveness. "No, not really."

Adam scowled. "When are you going to start living again, Erin? How long are you going to let one mistake ruin your life?"

"Not just one mistake," she reminded him. "The last one almost got Chelsea hurt. I'm not going to risk that again."

"Not all men are like Martin and Scott, you know. There are plenty of decent guys who like kids."

"Yeah. Well, I don't seem to do a very good job of finding them, do I?"

"Dammit, Erin, you're a young, beautiful woman. You shouldn't be so alone."

"I'm not alone, Adam. I have Chelsea. And I have you."

"And what about *you*? You don't even know who you are anymore. It's as if your own needs don't even exist."

"I know exactly who I am," she replied evenly. "I'm Chelsea's mom."

"Dammit, Erin—"

Whatever else he might have said was cut off by the telephone. She gulped and shut her eyes. *Oh, no! Not tonight. Adam will never understand.*

"Aren't you going to get that?"

Her eyes flew open to find him staring at the ringing phone on the end table right by his elbow. If only she'd turned on her answering machine. But, of course, Adam knew that she almost never kept it on when she was home, preferring to answer calls herself. He'd still suspect something. "Of course. I—uh—"

"Slow tonight, aren't you?" He reached for the receiver.

"No!"

But Erin's lunge was too late. His eyes narrowing suspiciously at her behavior, Adam spoke determinedly into the phone. "Yeah?"

Erin hovered beside him. She should have known. For some reason, she'd never been able to keep a secret from Adam.

"Yeah," Adam said again. "This is 555-2029. Who'd you want to speak to?"

He wouldn't know who to ask for, Erin suddenly realized. He didn't know her name. She could imagine him stumbling for an answer to Adam's less-than-gracious question. "Adam, give me the phone," she ordered, holding out her hand.

He scowled, but placed the receiver in her palm.

"Thank you," she told him, closing her fingers around the plastic instrument. She lifted it to her ear. "Hello?"

"Look, I can call another time," her caller said apologetically. "I didn't know you had company. I felt like a real idiot when he asked who I wanted to talk to."

Even with the awkwardness of the circumstances, she was warmed by his deep, rich voice, as always. "It's all right," she assured him quietly. "It's my brother, Adam."

She wondered if she only imagined that his voice lightened several degrees in what almost seemed like relief when he spoke again. "Oh, I thought maybe you'd found a likely prospect for that affair you're looking for."

"I told you I'm *not* looking," she replied gruffly, turning her back to her brother, who made no pretense of giving her privacy for the call. "And, don't you ever think about anything else?"

His husky chuckle reverberated through the receiver, causing a faint ripple of response to course down her spine. "Honey, it's been two and a half months since I've even been on a date. I'm afraid I've become a bit preoccupied with that subject lately."

Erin couldn't think of anything to say. Had Adam not been listening, she would have made some teasing remark about her friend's continuing complaints about his lack of a love life. After all, they'd gotten into the habit of saying whatever popped into their minds. But Adam *was* listening—intently—and she couldn't do that. So she said instead, rather inanely, "How's your sister?"

He laughed at last. "I take it your brother's listening."

"Yes."

"Does he know about me?"

"No."

"Going to tell him?"

"No."

"Why not?"

"I— Because."

He didn't sound particularly pleased. "Oh, come on. It's not as if you have anything to hide. We're friends. And don't you think it's about time we started showing it? Tell me your name."

Her eyes widened. "No!"

He paused. "Because Adam's listening?" he asked after a moment.

"No."

"You mean you have no intention of *ever* telling me?" he asked incredulously.

"Look, we agreed." Her voice sounded thin, her hands were inexplicably damp. She fought to appear calm, though she knew how little chance she had of fooling Adam—no more than he'd had of hiding that new scar at his temple.

Her caller cursed beneath his breath. "We agreed not to meet. I thought the name thing was just an amusing game that we'd get tired of after a while and stop playing. But you weren't playing, were you? You never intended for me to know who you are."

"N-no," she admitted.

"So you really have just been using me for some sort of therapy," he said slowly, as if he hadn't really believed it until now. "Maybe a cheap thrill or two. Sorry I never gave you more of a rush. If you'd told me you wanted telephone thrills, I'd have made a few really obscene calls. You know—a bit of heavy breathing, followed by asking you what you're wearing."

Her fingers tightened on the receiver until they went numb. She chewed her lip, wondering how to beg him not to do this without having Adam snatch the phone from her hand and demand to know what was going on. If she didn't know better, she'd swear she heard pain in that deep, likable voice—almost as if she had hurt him.

"Look, I've got to go. I must have lost my mind to think that I could really become friends with someone over the telephone."

"No! Wait, please!" The words were torn from her throat. "Don't hang up—" But she didn't know what to call him. And it didn't matter, anyway, because he'd already slammed his receiver home.

"Damn," she muttered, hanging up her own phone. She kept her back turned to her brother, postponing the inevitable.

She'd known he wouldn't give her long and he didn't. "Who the hell was that?"

"Has it even crossed your mind that it's none of your business?" she asked quietly.

"Look, Erin, something strange was going on just now and I want to know what," he responded curtly. Overprotective brother on the job. "Who was that?"

Maybe her caller had been right. Maybe they'd both lost their minds. All of a sudden, the relationship they'd built over the past two months began to seem very odd. Crossing her arms defensively at her waist, Erin turned slowly to Adam. Adam, who'd always taken care of her. Adam, who always had the answers. Adam, who would never enter a relationship without knowing all the details.

"I don't know who it is," she told him, steeling herself for his reaction.

Adam rose deliberately to his feet. "You *what?*"

"I don't know who it is," she repeated more firmly. "Sit back down and I'll tell you about it."

"Have you lost your mind?" Adam almost yelled some five minutes later — familiar-sounding words. He was standing again, his hands on his lean hips as he loomed over the chair in which Erin huddled. "You've been having phone conversations with a total stranger whose name you don't even know? Just what the hell have you told this guy?"

"Nothing, really." *Only things I've never told anyone else—not even you, my dear, angry brother.*

"Does he know who you are?" The words came at her like bullets.

She exhaled impatiently. "No. I told you—neither of us knows who the other is. Only phone numbers and cities."

"Does he know about Chelsea?"

"No." *He doesn't even like children,* she thought sadly, though she knew better than to mention that right now. "Dammit, Adam, you know I wouldn't endanger Chelsea! If I thought there was any reason not to trust this man—"

"If you trusted him, then why didn't you tell him who you were?" Adam shot back.

Because I needed a fantasy and he fit the part beautifully. Because I was getting lonely and hadn't even realized it until he entered my life. And maybe I'm just a bit tired of always being responsible and careful and mature.

She said nothing.

"We'll have your phone number changed tomorrow," Adam announced grimly. "And you'll give me his number and I'll have it traced. I'll run a make on him, find out who the hell he is, what kind of game he's been playing."

"Now, wait a minute." Erin shoved herself defiantly out of the chair, standing up to her brother for one of the few times in her life. "You're not doing *any* of that, do you hear me? I'm not changing my number and I'm not giving you his. You're not running any makes on anyone. You're to stay out of it."

He probably wouldn't have looked more surprised if she'd punched him in the stomach. "Look, Erin, this is ridiculous. We're talking about your safety, here."

"Right. *My* safety." She lifted her chin even farther, matching her voice to his in volume. "I know I've come running to you plenty of times in the past, Adam, but this time I'm not asking for help. I've been on my own for four years now, wholly responsible for myself and my child, and I've learned to take care of myself during that time. I've also learned to make some decisions—maybe even some mistakes—and to take full responsibility for them."

She took a deep, steadying breath, then continued. "I won't pretend that I don't need someone to talk to at times. Obviously I do. But I don't need anyone telling me who I'll talk to on my own telephone, or screening the friends

I make on my own. Do you understand? Now, I may never talk to that man again. I don't know. But if I do, then the decision is mine and mine alone. Got that?"

"Dammit, Erin, this is crazy!" Adam exploded. "You need a real flesh-and-blood man in your life, not some imaginary lover. You can't keep hiding from life, afraid to take chances, substituting a nameless, faceless voice for a shoulder to lay your head on."

"I don't need a shoulder," she answered flatly. "I don't need anyone. Except you. I need you to accept me, Adam, and to accept my ability to take care of myself."

They stared at each other for what seemed like a very long time. Always, in the past, Erin's resolve had crumpled beneath Adam's more forceful one. Not this time. He seemed to realize that she wasn't going to give in. "On one condition," he said finally, apparently determined to be difficult to the end.

"What?" she asked warily.

"If you *ever* suspect that something's not quite right about the guy, you'll let me check him out."

"All right," she conceded, knowing his dictatorial behavior was prompted by genuine love and concern for her.

"Promise."

"I promise."

He nodded. "All right. Then I'll stay out of it."

"Thank you."

They didn't speak of it again until Erin announced an hour later that she was turning in, laying out sheets and blankets for Adam, who would sleep on the couch, which made into a bed.

"Hey, sis," he said as she headed for her room.

She paused in the doorway. "Yes?"

He stood beside the sofa bed with his hands in the pockets of his worn jeans, his hard, unreadable face as soft as she'd ever seen it, his dark-eyed gaze unusually warm as it rested on her face. "I may not like this telephone game of yours, but I have to admit it took spunk for you to stand up to me like that. I know I have a reputation for being a bit—intimidating."

"A bit," she murmured dryly.

He inclined his head in response, but went on: "You've come a long way since you were twenty-two. If Martin were to meet you for the first time now, I don't think he'd find you such an easy mark."

She smiled brightly, touched by the atypical praise. "Neither do I, Adam. Good night. And thanks."

"Good night, kid. Sleep well."

"HOW'D YOU LIKE THE MOVIE?"

"Um—oh, it was, er, what did you think?"

Brett tugged viciously at the buttons of his shirt, muttering beneath his breath as the scene from his disastrous date played through his mind. He'd known she wasn't exactly a potential Nobel prizewinner when he'd asked her out, but he hadn't realized that there was nothing between her ears but cotton candy. If she even had any opinions of her own, she'd kept them well hidden, choosing, instead, to defer to his.

Unlike the woman in Arkansas, who not only had opinions, but didn't mind expressing them. And what fascinating, stimulating opinions they were.

Dammit. Was he going to compare every date he had to a woman he'd never even met? How long was he going to remain celibate because no other woman appealed to his mind in quite the way she did, despite the needs of his body?

One didn't fall in love with a voice on the phone, he told himself sternly, tossing his rumpled shirt to the floor. It had turned out one couldn't even make friends over the telephone. So why couldn't he stop thinking about her ten days after that last, irritating conversation?

He missed her, dammit. And he'd never even known her name.

He looked at his watch. Ten-thirty. He hadn't been home from a date at ten-thirty since junior high, when all the girls had curfews. But he and Ms. Airhead had finally had to concede defeat and he'd taken her home. She'd seemed more relieved than insulted. All in all, his ego and his mood had taken quite a beating tonight.

When the phone rang he almost cringed. Surely not the woman he'd just taken home, he told himself, though he was afraid it would be. Maybe she wanted to apologize or demand an apology from him, or something equally uncomfortable. He wouldn't answer it. His machine would get it on the fourth ring.

The answering machine intercepted the call with its usual brisk efficiency, informing the caller that he/she had reached the home of Brett Nash, who was tied up at the moment and to please leave a message after the beep. Brett cocked his head, standing by the phone to listen to the message.

"Brett? So that's your name. Um—mine is Erin Spencer. And I'm very sorry I hurt you. Please call me."

He had the receiver to his ear before she finished speaking. He was surprised to note that his hand wasn't quite steady. "Don't hang up. I'm here, Erin."

4

ERIN HAD DECIDED Brett wasn't home when she heard the answering machine. She hadn't expected him to pick up the phone. When he did, her mind suddenly went blank. Just what was it she'd wanted to say? she asked herself frantically.

"Erin? Are you still there?"

"I'm here, Brett," she answered finally, his name sounding strange on her lips. Brett. Brett Nash. The man who'd somehow become her friend.

"So your name is Erin."

"Erin Spencer," she confirmed, wondering why they were talking so awkwardly now. It had never been like that before.

"Why did you suddenly decide to tell me?"

The faint suspicion in his voice told her that he hadn't forgotten their last conversation. "I've thought a lot about what you said," she confessed. "And I realized you were right. I was using you. You'd become an emotional outlet for me, a no-risk fantasy friend who expected nothing from me. I'm sorry, Brett. I never meant to hurt your feelings."

"I've missed you, Erin."

His simple statement brought a lump to her throat. "I've missed you, too. Can you forgive me?"

"Of course. I understand. Our friendship hasn't exactly been a conventional one."

"Not exactly," she agreed wryly.

"I consider you a friend. I enjoy talking to you. You make me laugh and think, and you're a great listener when I need to talk. You never seem to be bored by what I say. Just as I'm never bored when you talk. Unlike my date earlier this evening," he added with a rueful sigh.

Warmed by his sincere-sounding praise, Erin chuckled at his last words. "You've been on a date tonight? Not a successful one, I take it, since you're home so early."

"Not successful at all." He launched into an exaggerated account of his miserable evening, making her laugh again and again. It was the first time she'd felt like laughing since their quarrel ten days earlier.

"I'm really sorry about your evening," she commiserated when he finished. "It sounds dreadful."

"It was," he assured her. "I'm getting desperate here, Erin. I may yet have to come to Arkansas and seduce you with flowers and flattery."

As she had in the past, Erin brushed off his suggestion, immediately changing the subject by asking about his sister. Which led to him asking about Adam. "Is he still visiting you?"

"Oh, no. He was only here for a couple of days. He couldn't take much time away from his job."

"What is it he does, exactly? You said he works for the government?"

"He's a DEA agent," Erin informed him, waiting for the usual reaction.

Brett gave a low whistle. "Whew. Tough job. Dangerous, too."

"Yes, it is. That's why I worry about him so much."

"Does he like his work?"

"I guess he does, since he's still doing it."

"Did you ever tell him about me?"

Erin winced. "He knows."

As if sensing something in her voice, he spoke quickly. "He doesn't approve?"

"He tends to be overprotective," Erin explained carefully. "He—uh—he didn't really understand."

Brett was silent for a moment. "I guess I can see his point. I'd feel kind of funny if it were my sister talking repeatedly to a stranger."

"Cheryl's married, isn't she?" Erin asked, wanting to distract Brett from her brother's reservations.

"Yeah."

"Any children?"

"Two. Little monsters, the both of them." He sounded indulgently amused. "Every time I'm around them I thank the stars they're hers instead of mine."

At this new reminder of Brett's attitude toward children, Erin abruptly changed the subject. "So what movie did you see tonight?"

He named a recent release that had received quite a bit of publicity because of a steamy love scene between the two stars. "The movie was okay," he commented. "Not great, but okay."

"I saw it last week with a friend from work."

This time she knew she didn't imagine the meaningful pause before he asked in an unsuccessful attempt at casualness, "A girlfriend?"

"Yes. So what did you think of the notorious love scene in the middle?"

"I thought it was the best part of the movie, actually. Beautifully filmed and acted. Very sensual. I kept thinking what a shame it was I was seeing it with a woman who didn't interest me in the slightest."

She didn't like thinking of him on a date with another woman any more than he apparently cared for the thought of her with another man. She was going to have to think about that more carefully later, she decided. "It *was* a nice scene, wasn't it?" she remarked almost absently. "Using the amber filter was very effective. It made the scene dreamy—a nice contrast to the gritty reality of the main story line. As you said, it's too bad the rest of the film didn't stand up."

Brett responded with the husky chuckle that always made her smile. "You really are a sucker for romance, aren't you? Quite the traditionalist."

"I suppose so," she answered slowly. "Maybe because I've never really known the type of romance poets and novelists write about. It probably doesn't even exist, but it does make wonderful fantasy material."

"It exists, Erin. You just haven't found the guy to share it with yet."

"Spoken like another true romantic," she teased, keeping her tone light.

"You know, I didn't think I was a romantic until fairly recently. Now I'm beginning to believe I am."

"Oh?" Disturbed by the new intensity in his voice, she asked without thinking, "When did you come to this amazing conclusion?"

"When I found myself falling for a voice on the telephone," he replied.

The words made her tremble. How serious had he been? Was he only teasing, or . . . ?

"Um—" She swallowed, her fingers tightening on the receiver. "Gosh, it's getting late, isn't it?" she commented lamely.

"Yeah, I guess it is," he agreed, and he sounded patiently understanding. "We'll talk again, Erin."

It wasn't a question, but she answered it, anyway. "Yes. We will. Good night, Brett."

"Good night, Erin Spencer. Did I remember to tell you what a beautiful name that is?"

She couldn't help smiling. "Thank you."

"No." His voice deepened. "Thank *you*, Erin. Good night."

She hung up slowly, her hand lingering on the receiver as if reluctant to break the contact with Brett. She closed her eyes, wondering exactly what she'd just done. There was no more pretending that Brett was simply a fantasy friend, an outlet for anonymous conversations and a bit of harmless fun. He had a name now. He'd become real.

She should have known this would happen if the calls continued. She was too old for imaginary friends. Reality had been destined to intrude. She never should have encouraged him to keep calling. But he had. And now they knew each other's names. And he would call again. And again, until he grew tired of talking to her and found a more satisfactory relationship in Boston, or until he demanded something more from her. Like a face-to-face meeting.

The thought of actually meeting Brett still paralyzed her. As Adam had pointed out, there was something rather strange going on between Erin and Brett—a bond that shouldn't have developed, a connection with the potential to hurt if severed. Look how much she'd missed just talking to him in the past ten days. How much more would she miss after meeting him and then being disappointed in him, having this special friendship change or—more likely—end?

She didn't doubt that she would be disappointed. No one could be as perfect as the fantasy friend she'd created in Brett during the past few months. No man could be as patient, as understanding, as caring as he'd seemed. As much as she loved her brother, she couldn't even imagine living with him for an extended period. Brett was charming enough during telephone calls, but she knew too well how familiarity bred contempt.

And besides, she reminded herself, Brett had just as idealized an image of her. He'd admitted that he imagined her as a beautiful woman—a sleeping beauty, of sorts, only waiting for the right man to come along and seduce her back to life. A woman as footloose and unencumbered as he was, able to drop everything on a whim and go looking for fun. He didn't know that she was, primarily, Chelsea's mom. That the Erin he'd come to know was a pretense created to add a bit of excitement to her life. Someone he'd never been meant to meet.

She was satisfied with the way things were now, she tried to convince herself as she prepared for bed. Why risk messing things up by changing them?

ERIN SPENCER. Such a beautiful name. Lying in his bed, hands behind his head, Brett grinned into the darkness. She'd trusted him enough to tell him her name.

And then his smile faded. That was all she'd trusted him with, he reminded himself. There were still many things he didn't know about Erin. Chief among them why she was so terrified of the idea of meeting him.

She was becoming more intriguing, more important to him by the day. Whatever this was between them shouldn't have developed, logically. And yet it had, and it couldn't be ignored or denied. Their meeting was inevitable. He would probably have to take matters into his own hands to make sure that meeting occurred. Because he was terribly afraid his life would continue to revolve around a voice on the telephone until he made some effort to get over his obsession with her—even if it took a face-to-face meeting to do so.

And there was always a chance—a very slim, very fragile, very precious chance—that what they'd found during an accidental telephone call had been something that would last them a lifetime.

"AND HE *LOVES* KIDS. After all, he has four of his own. So what do you think, Erin?"

Erin looked up from the paperwork she'd been scanning, straightening her reading glasses on her nose. "What did you say, Eileen?"

The petite copywriter sighed and threw her hands in the air. "You weren't even listening! I was telling you about a wo-o-n-derful, definitely available man and you weren't even paying attention. My cousin, Bill. He's attractive, nice, loaded and single. So why don't I fix the two of you up for a date?"

"A date?"

Eileen grimaced again. "Honestly, Erin. Sometimes I worry about you. A date. You know—a man and a woman going out for dinner? Maybe a movie? Maybe a lifetime commitment? Surely you remember the custom."

Erin couldn't help but laugh at Eileen's disgusted expression. "Yes, I vaguely remember dates," she admitted.

"Great. Then you'll do it?"

"No." Erin spoke gently, but quite firmly.

Eileen exhaled, her never-idle hands swinging into motion again. "Why not?"

"Because I also happen to remember the custom of blind dates. They are almost always awkward, painful, embarrassing, degrading and generally disastrous. Thank you very much, but I'd just as soon pass on that particular pleasure."

"Believe me, I know about blind dates. I've had a few nightmares after them myself."

"Good. Then you understand why I have to decline."

Eileen shook her red head vigorously. "No, I don't. There's always hope. And Bill's different. He's a really nice guy."

"That's what they all say." Erin smiled to soften her refusal. "Sorry. Not interested." She reached out to gather the specs for her latest free-lance assignment from Redding & Howard, the advertising agency where Eileen worked full-time. "Is this everything?"

"Yeah." But Eileen wasn't quite ready to drop the subject or Erin's social life—or lack thereof. "I just don't understand it. You're drop-dead gorgeous. You have a figure I'd kill for. You've got a great personality. It's so depressing that I sometimes wonder why I even like you. And yet you live the life of an elderly widow. Why?"

"Let's just say I quit while I was relatively ahead," Erin answered with a faint smile. "I have Chelsea. She's enough to make me happy."

"And what are you going to have when Chelsea grows up and leaves home?" Eileen demanded sternly, hands on her rounded hips. "An empty house, that's what," she answered before Erin could speak. "Are you still going to be happy then?"

"Eileen, I haven't ruled out all future relationships," Erin pointed out. "I'm just not interested in going on a blind date."

She was half-tempted to tell Eileen about Brett—her regular "blind telephone date." She didn't, of course. She didn't expect anyone to understand about Brett. Except Corey, perhaps. She was seriously considering talking to Corey about her confusion where Brett was concerned next time Corey called. Corey had always had a different perspective on things than most people, and Erin had always valued her friend's opinions more than anyone else's—with the exception, perhaps, of Adam's.

"Okay," Eileen conceded reluctantly. "No blind dates. But how about if I give a party sometime—a party with lots of people there—and invite both you and Bill. Would you come, just to meet him? It wouldn't be a date or anything, just a social occasion. Would you accept then?"

"Maybe. I'll think about it," Erin promised. Placing her glasses in her purse, she gathered the paperwork for the assignment, impatient to get home and get to work. "Thanks for caring, Eileen," she added, knowing that the other woman's compulsive matchmaking was motivated by genuine concern. "I'll see you Friday."

She thought a great deal about Eileen's offer during the drive from the downtown Little Rock ad agency across the Arkansas River to her home in the adjacent city of North Little Rock. She hadn't even been tempted to agree to the blind date. True, she'd never cared for dates arranged in that manner, but for some reason she wasn't entirely sure she'd turned Eileen down just because of that. It was wholly illogical, of course, but for just a moment when Eileen had made the suggestion, Erin had felt almost . . . guilty, she decided uncomfortably. Disloyal. As if she were a woman committed to a monogamous relationship, not free to be listening to offers of dates with other men.

Ridiculous, she told herself, tightening her fingers on the steering wheel of her car. It was so foolish that thoughts of Brett had crossed her mind at that moment. She was hardly committed in that way to Brett. She'd never even met the man! So why in the world had she suddenly allowed her life to revolve around those continuing telephone calls?

No, she corrected herself immediately. Her life didn't revolve around those calls. Parking in front of her neat white-frame house, she reached to the passenger seat for her battered leather portfolio. Chelsea was the center of her life, followed closely by her brother, her friends and her work. Brett fell somewhere into the category of friend. Like Corey and Eileen and . . .

She winced, slamming her car door in a futile effort to deny the awareness that Brett was like no one else in her life. He was becoming entirely too important to her. And she didn't for the life of her know what she was going to do about it.

"Mommy, Mommy! Look what Mrs. Price made for me!"

Erin turned with a smile in response to her daughter's voice. Chelsea ran toward her from the yard next door, where she'd been staying with their neighbor while Erin ran her errands. She clutched a new rag doll of white muslin with brown yarn braids, a red flowered cotton dress and an endearing embroidered face. "What an adorable doll!"

"She's mine! Mrs. Price made her for me on the sewing machine. And she gave her brown hair and brown eyes, just like me. Isn't she beautiful, Mommy?"

"Very," Erin agreed solemnly. She looked at the smiling woman who'd followed Chelsea across the yard. "That was very sweet of you, Isabelle. Thank you."

The older woman beamed from behind her silver-framed glasses, one fragile hand resting on Chelsea's shoulder. "You know how I enjoy making things," she replied. "I found this pattern the other day and I couldn't resist making one for Chelsea. I hoped she'd like it."

"I love her," Chelsea breathed, hugging the doll tightly. "I'm going to name her Belle—after you, Mrs. Price. Is that all right?"

"I'd like that very much. You can keep her a long time and think about me every time you play with her."

"I will," Chelsea promised. "Always."

Erin regarded her daughter. How Chelsea would have loved Erin's mother, who'd died when Erin was only a teenager. Martin's mother, too, had died years earlier. Mrs. Price had become a substitute for the grandmother Chelsea had never had but always wanted. Erin was grateful to have found such a dependable, loving and willing baby-sitter for the few times she left the house without Chelsea.

She wanted so much for Chelsea to have everything she desired. She realized she was actually beginning to feel guilty because she couldn't provide her daughter with a grandmother. Wearily, Erin wondered if guilt had always been such an intrinsic part of motherhood, or whether she had a corner on that particular market. "Thanks for watching her, Isabelle. And for the doll. I know she'll treasure her."

"I'm going to go show Belle my room," Chelsea announced, running for the front door. "And she needs to meet my other dolls."

"Just a minute, sweetheart, I haven't unlocked the door yet," Erin called after her, sharing an amused look with her neighbor.

"I won't keep you. Chelsea's excited and you look like you have work to do." Isabelle eyed the bulging portfolio under Erin's arm.

"Yes, thank goodness. The bills will be paid for another month."

Isabelle chuckled and started toward her own house. "See you later, Erin."

"Hurry, Mommy! Belle wants to go in."

Erin smiled. How could she ever have thought there was something missing from her life? She gazed lovingly at her flushed daughter. Chelsea was all she needed, all she wanted. She couldn't wish for anything more. And she wouldn't allow herself to dwell on the most disquieting question Eileen had asked—a question that had hovered ominously at the back of Erin's mind ever since.

What are you going to have when Chelsea grows up and leaves home?

CHELSEA WAS SETTLED for the night, sleeping peacefully with Belle tucked tightly in the curve of one arm, when Erin finally had a chance to relax. She'd worked all afternoon while Chelsea had played with her new doll, stopping only to have dinner with her daughter and then watch television with her for an hour before bedtime. And then she'd worked for another hour.

Putting one hand to the small of her back, Erin stretched, wincing at the protest of muscles that had been frozen in one position for too long. Hand cramping, she set down her drawing pencil. She was tired. Her eyes burned behind the glasses she wore for reading and close work. They felt strained. She'd been meaning to make an appointment with her optometrist for months. She'd better do it soon, she thought wearily. For now, she needed rest.

She'd just slipped into her nightgown and crawled into bed when the telephone rang. Her energy returned as if by magic. Eagerly, she lifted the receiver of the bedside extension. "Hello?"

"Hi."

Erin curled beneath the covers, making herself comfortable for a long, cozy conversation. "Hello, Brett." His name still felt rather strange on her lips. This was only the third time she'd talked to him since they'd exchanged names.

"Are you busy? Can you talk now?"

"Of course," she agreed promptly. "I just put my work away for the night. I was getting ready for bed."

A noticeable pause followed her words. When Brett spoke, his voice sounded rather strained. "So—uh—what have you been working on? You know, you've never told me exactly what you do."

"I'm a commercial artist," she replied, no longer bothering with evasions. After all, he knew her name. The only part of her life she still felt compelled to keep from him was her daughter. For some reason, she couldn't bring herself to tell him about Chelsea. She didn't try to analyze her reasons. "I free-lance for some local advertising agencies."

"Really?" He sounded genuinely interested. "Another amazing coincidence. Our relationship has been filled with them, hasn't it?"

Her attention was caught briefly by the word *relationship*. She decided not to think about that, either. "You're a commercial artist, too?"

"In a way. I write a comic book. I don't suppose you've ever heard of *The Midnight Warrior*?"

She frowned. "No," she admitted. "I haven't. But I'm not very familiar with comic books. Only *Superman*."

"Ah, well, don't apologize. It's fairly new. I've only been writing it for two years. It's doing very well, though. There's talk about picking it up for a Saturday-morning cartoon."

"Wow!" She was impressed and didn't hide it. "I've never known anyone who wrote a comic book before. You do the artwork, too?"

"Yep. It's a hobby turned career obsession. Believe it or not, I used to be a stockbroker."

"Somehow I can't imagine you as a stockbroker," she said with a laugh. Comic-book author seemed much more suitable for the offbeat, funny, impulsive man she'd come to know, and despite the similarities of their professions, emblematic of the differences between them. Her artwork was practical, functional, meant to sell products; Brett lived in a fantasy world of his own creation. "Tell me about *The Midnight Warrior*."

He launched into a sheepishly enthusiastic description of his hero, a vigilante who dispensed justice and retribution in an unnamed big city. Yes, he admitted, it was violent in typical comic-book fashion, but it also upheld old-fashioned values. "I'm not trying to moralize to my young readers," he added, "but I hope my hero's clear-cut sense of right and wrong serves as a positive influence against the evils of crime and drugs."

"I'm going to buy one of your comic books tomorrow," Erin promised him, smiling. "I can't wait to read one."

"It's not exactly written for adult women," Brett warned. "The stories appeal mostly to adolescent boys."

"I'm still going to read them. I'd like to know more about how your mind works."

He laughed. "You should talk to my sister. She has some very interesting theories on that subject. Most of them to my disadvantage, I'm afraid."

"She's a sister. It's her job to keep you cut down to size," Erin teased.

"Is that what you do with your brother?"

Erin thought ruefully of Adam. "As much as anyone could, I suppose."

They talked about their respective jobs for another half hour. And then Brett yawned in the middle of a sentence. "Sorry," he apologized. "It's been a long day at the drawing board."

Erin grimaced in empathy. "I know the feeling."

"I'm beat."

"Yeah. Me, too."

"You know what I'd really like to do now?" Brett asked after a pause.

She snuggled more deeply into her pillow, cradling the telephone to her ear. "Get some sleep?" she hazarded.

"Eventually. But first I'd like to build a fire, put on some music—Rachmaninoff, I think—pour some wine—no, better yet, hot chocolate, with marshmallows—and curl up on a soft sofa. With you."

She caught her breath, then swallowed. "That sounds lovely," she said casually. "But I guess you'd better settle for a hot bath and a good night's rest."

"I want to see you, Erin. The calls aren't enough anymore."

His words had caught her off guard. She could have cried. Why had he done this to them tonight, after such a pleasantly undemanding conversation. Why was he putting this pressure on her? Why couldn't he understand that what they had was too important to her to take a chance on losing it? "Brett—"

"Dammit, Erin. I'm human, you know? I need more in my life than a disembodied voice."

"Then find someone," she told him, though the words were difficult to push past the lump in her throat. "There must be hundreds of eligible women in Boston."

"I've tried that, remember? I can't stop thinking about you."

"Brett, you don't even know me." She looked at the picture of Chelsea on the nightstand beside the phone, and her vision blurred with tears.

"We can remedy that. I want to meet you, Erin. Face-to-face."

She closed her eyes, willing the tears away. "We'll...we'll talk about it some other time, all right? It's late tonight. We're both tired."

His sigh carried clearly through the lines. "Time isn't going to change anything."

"Brett, I—"

"I'm lonely, Erin. Can't you understand that?" The question was asked quietly, deeply, almost reluctantly. As if he'd had to swallow a healthy amount of masculine pride to make the admission.

Her bed seemed suddenly large and empty, her house all too quiet. She thought of sitting on a couch in front of a fire, sipping hot chocolate with someone who cared about her. Really cared. And she yearned. "Yes, Brett," she whispered. "I understand."

"Then—"

"Please. Not tonight. I'm just not ready to discuss this tonight. I'm so tired." Tired. Upset. Frightened. A little annoyed with him for pushing her this way. And so very confused.

"All right," he conceded quietly. "But we'll talk about it again. You know that, don't you?"

"I— Good night, Brett."

"Good night, Erin. Sweet dreams."

She already knew what her dreams would be, and set the receiver in its cradle. She knew that she'd wake flushed and frustrated, with Brett's husky voice echoing in her mind.

She suspected it would be a long while before she slept that night.

BRETT SLAMMED his own receiver down so hard the telephone jingled in protest. "Dammit!"

He shouldn't have pushed her. He hadn't meant to—hadn't even planned to mention a meeting tonight when he'd called her. The words had slipped out before he could stop them.

He needed to see her. To touch her. To find out if the woman he'd come to know and care about was real. He was a man with normal male appetites, and desire was beginning to eat a hole in his gut. If only he could find someone else to dull that hunger. The problem was that his hunger was a very specific one. No other woman interested him; no other woman intrigued him the way Erin did.

And he'd never even seen her.

Dammit, he thought again. Something had to give. He couldn't go on this way.

Meeting her would accomplish one of two things. Either he'd discover once and for all that he and Erin could never be more than friends and he'd be able to get back to a normal social life, or...

Considering the ramifications of that "or" had him breaking out in a cold sweat. It could be that he and Erin would be dynamite together.

Fantasies came easily to a man in his business. He could almost see himself with her, though he wished he had more than a hazy image of the woman in his daydreams. He imagined meeting her, of a spark of physical attraction as strong and immediate as the mental bond that had developed during that first telephone call. He pictured the two of them on outings, sharing the films and concerts they both enjoyed, dining on the Italian and Chinese cuisines they'd both claimed as favorites.

Carrying the fantasy even further, he thought of having her with him in Boston. Showing her around his city, strolling hand in hand through the Common, visiting the aquarium, spending an evening at his favorite Irish pub. Just the two of them. And, afterward . . . Well, anything was possible.

He was a normal man with a normal man's needs, a normal man's dreams. He needed someone to share his life with. Someone special. Someone real. Someone who could very well be Erin Spencer.

He had to meet her. One way or another, he would.

5

"SO MEET HER."

"Yeah, sure." Brett cradled the receiver against his shoulder and scowled at his feet, which were crossed on the desk in front of him. Cheryl tended to oversimplify things, he reflected, even as he told her, "It's not that easy."

"Sure, it is. You just walk up to her and say, 'Hi, I'm here. Let's get married.'"

Brett chuckled at his sister's teasing. Cheryl had been fascinated when he'd told her about Erin, amused by the series of telephone calls that had all started when he'd misdialed her number one stormy evening. He'd asked her, only half-hopefully, if she knew anyone named Erin Spencer. She didn't, but thought Erin sounded delightful. She asserted that it was time Brett met the woman who'd captured his attention so thoroughly.

"Cheryl, she doesn't want to meet me. I think she's concerned that it wouldn't work out, that the circumstances of our knowing each other are too strange."

"What's so strange about it?" Cheryl demanded. "It's no different than meeting through the mail, like those lonely-hearts-club things. Lots of people meet over the phone."

Brett privately agreed. He was beginning to wonder exactly what lay behind Erin's panic at the thought of seeing him. She wasn't going to tell him. There was only one way for him to find out. He had to meet her. "So, you think I should ignore her objections and meet her, anyway?" he asked his sister, wondering why he felt the need of reassurance on a decision that was, in effect, already made.

"You bet I do. I'm ready for a sister-in-law and some nieces and nephews. And Dad's starting to get anxious for grandsons bearing the family name."

"Yes, I know," Brett agreed dryly, thinking of his last conversation with his father—the old speech about Brett being the last of the line unless he got busy and had some sons. His father was the old-fashioned type, big on traditions. Brett hadn't acknowledged then that for the past several years he'd been subconsciously searching for someone to share his life. He knew now that he had been, though he hadn't given serious thought to the quest until he'd started talking to Erin.

"But, Cheryl, Erin may be right," he felt compelled to point out. "We may *not* hit it off in person. Maybe we're only meant to remain telephone friends."

"Why shouldn't you hit it off in person when you've been talking for months?" she returned logically. "Usually couples run into trouble when an initial physical attraction pales and they find themselves unable to talk. You and Erin shouldn't have that problem—you already know so much about each other. You have so much more in common than physical attraction. Of course, there is the chance that you won't find her attractive," she added reflectively.

He rejected that immediately. "It doesn't matter what she looks like. She still fascinates me more than any woman I've ever known."

"Well, hallelujah. Maybe there's hope for you, after all. How many times have I told you that if you'd quit chasing after empty-headed beauty queens, you just might find someone special?"

Not another I-told-you-so speech, Brett thought with a scowl. "That was a bigoted remark, Cheryl. Who said a woman can't be beautiful *and* intelligent? Might I point out that there are those misguided persons who find *you* appealing? You're no airhead, either. Most of the time."

"Why, Brett. That was almost a compliment. Thank you."

"It might turn out the other way around, you know. Erin may not be attracted to me. I'm hardly the male-model type."

"That's ridiculous," Cheryl responded instantly, loyally. "You're a very cute guy. Any woman with any taste would appreciate you."

Grimacing at the hated word *cute*, Brett quickly changed the subject. "All this is really academic, anyway. Erin doesn't want to meet me. She's not going to agree if I try to set something up."

"Hmm. That could be a problem." Cheryl was quiet for a few moments, then he could almost hear the snap of her fingers. "I've got it!"

"What?" he asked warily.

"Meet her without telling her!"

He frowned. "I beg your pardon?"

"You know—don't tell her who you are. You can meet her incognito. That way she'll have a chance to get to know and like you without freezing up."

"Cheryl, that's ridiculous. I couldn't do that."

"Why not? Tell her your name is—oh, B.J. After all, that was your nickname in school. Since she won't have any artificial expectations from a total stranger, you'll have time to charm her into giving you a real chance."

Brett was drawn into the fantasy despite his better judgment. "She'd recognize my voice."

"From telephone conversations? Hardly. Half your best friends don't recognize your voice over the phone. You're one of those people who sound different in person. Besides," she added enthusiastically, warming to the plan, "Erin wouldn't be expecting to see you, which would make her even less likely to notice familiarities in your speech. What do you think?"

"I think you're nuts," he told her flatly.

She only laughed. "It could be fun."

"Uh-huh. And Erin could go for my throat when she finds out the truth. How would you like it if some guy did that to you?"

"I think it sounds very romantic," Cheryl answered loftily. "And it's similar to what Dwayne did with me, remember? Someone told him I wouldn't date cops, so he just didn't tell me he was one until after I'd been out with him a few times. By that time I was already hooked."

And then she gasped in exaggerated excitement. "Dwayne can help us find her! He can find out where she lives, whether she's ever been arrested for anything—"

"Cheryl," Brett interrupted, "you're insane. But, thanks. You've cheered me up considerably."

"Think about it, Brett. Okay? You really should meet her. Even if you don't like my plan of going undercover. Also, it gives you an excuse to visit me for a few days, which I've been nagging you to do for ages, anyway. Right?"

"Maybe," he temporized. "I've got to go to New York for a couple of days for my monthly meeting with my publisher. I'll think about it then and let you know what I decide."

Brett was still chuckling over Cheryl's wild plan later that evening as he dialed Erin's number. Meet Erin incognito. Only his nutty sister could have come up with that one. It was earlier than he usually called, but he'd waited as long as he could. He wanted to talk to Erin.

He warmed, as always, when her voice came through the line. "Hi. It's me," he murmured, settling back for another pleasantly frustrating conversation.

"Oh. Hi, Brett. Would you mind if I call you back a little later? I'm—um—kind of busy now."

He scowled, but answered graciously enough. "Of course. I plan to be here for the rest of the evening."

"All right. I'll call after eight, okay? My time," she added.

"Yeah, sure. Talk to you then." He hung up in frustration, wondering what was making her too busy to talk to him. He'd had the impression that she wasn't alone. *A date?* he wondered, hating the idea of another man being with Erin when he was so far away from her.

And then he took some hope in remembering that she'd promised to call after eight. If she was with a man, at least he wouldn't be staying the night.

He really was going to have to do something about this. They simply couldn't go on this way.

"WHO WAS THAT, Mommy? Uncle Adam?" Chelsea asked curiously as Erin hung up the phone.

"No, it wasn't Uncle Adam. It was just a friend. Now, finish your peas so you can have your bath before bedtime." Erin tried to keep her voice light, hoping to distract Chelsea from the telephone call before there were any more awkward questions.

Brett had never called that early before. She hoped he wasn't going to make a habit of calling before Chelsea's bedtime. What if Chelsea had picked up the phone or called out to her during the brief call? How would Erin have explained why she'd never told Brett about her daughter when she wasn't even quite sure, herself, why she'd been keeping that particular secret?

He hadn't much liked her putting him off. She bit her lip, wondering why she suddenly felt she owed him explanations. She didn't owe him anything. Right? After all, it wasn't as if they were involved in a relationship or anything. Well, not exactly. Sort of. Oh, she was getting a headache just thinking about it.

"What's wrong, Mommy?" Chelsea questioned, looking up from the peas she'd been pushing around her Garfield plate.

Erin hadn't realized she'd moaned aloud. "Nothing, sweetie. I was just thinking."

"About what?"

"Stop stalling and finish those peas," Erin ordered, changing the subject yet again.

She'd just gotten Chelsea into bed later that evening when the telephone rang again. She sighed. He really was getting very impatient. Lifting the receiver, she said without preamble, "I was just about to call you. I promise."

A moment of silence greeted her words. And then a familiar, obviously amused voice replied, "Well, that's really nice. Tell me, Erin, when did you take up ESP? A new hobby?"

Erin laughed. "Corey?"

"What? You mean you didn't already know, after all?"

"No. I thought you were someone else."

"Ah. So just who *is* this someone else? Someone I should know about?"

"Possibly."

"So talk, pal. Tell me all about him."

"How do you know it's a him?" Erin countered, wondering where to begin.

"It had to be. And I can't wait to hear the details. I thought you were never going to start dating again."

"Look who's talking. I'm not the one holed up in the Ozarks. When's the last time you had a date?"

"The night I came home black-and-blue from wrestling with Juan-the-Latin-lover-insurance-salesman six months ago," Corey answered candidly. "I decided to rest up awhile before the next match. Enough about me. Tell me about *him*."

Erin did. From the beginning. Including a few of the things she'd purposefully neglected to mention to Adam. Like the way she was beginning to plan her days around Brett's calls. The way her pulse went into double time at the sound of his voice. The emptiness she felt whenever he hung up and she heard nothing but a dial tone from the receiver. His growing insistence on a face-to-face meeting.

"So what's holding you back?"

Erin had hoped Corey would understand. "Corey, weren't you listening? He doesn't even like children."

"Of course he likes children. Erin, he writes comic books. Who do you think makes up his audience?"

"So, he likes them from a distance. That was what he said when I asked him."

"All guys say that. It's macho, or something. I'm sure he'd love Chelsea. Anyone but a low-life creep like your ex-husband would love her. Even your spooky brother is nutty about her, right? Or so you've said."

Erin laughed again, always amused by Corey's frankness. "Adam isn't spooky."

"Couldn't prove it by me. I've never met the guy, remember? He sneaks into your house in the middle of the night, then wraps his trench coat around him and slips back out again before anyone can see him. If I didn't know better, I'd swear he was a figment of your imagination. But we're not talking about your brother. We're talking about Brett. When are you going to meet him?"

"I don't know." There'd been a time when she'd have said never. Now the meeting was beginning to seem inevitable. She wasn't sure how much longer she could stall him. "I'm scared, Corey."

"Of what?" Corey asked, no longer teasing.

"Of being hurt again. Of having Chelsea hurt again. If I thought Brett and I could just get together for drinks or dinner, have a good time together and then go our own ways... But I'm afraid it would be more complicated than that. Much more complicated."

"You may be right. You could fall in love with the man. And he with you. And would that be so terrible?"

"It might be for Chelsea. I have to think of her first, Corey. Surely you understand that. She shouldn't have to suffer because her mother has such rotten luck with romance."

"Erin, you know I think you're a wonderful mother— the best. But you have to take care of your own needs, as well. You can't put your own life on hold until Chelsea's grown."

"Yes, I can, if I think it's best for her," Erin countered. "I'm all she has."

"And you punish yourself every day because Martin doesn't want her. It's not your fault, Erin. You've more than compensated for her selfish slimeball of a father."

Erin sighed and ran a hand through her disheveled hair. "We've spent your whole long-distance call talking about my problems. I haven't even asked about you. How are you, Corey?"

"I'm fine. I really like it here. It's very peaceful. Exactly what I needed for a while."

"And the shop?"

"In the black last month," Corey announced proudly. "By almost a dollar eighty-nine."

"I want to come see it sometime."

"I'd love for you to. Anytime."

They talked a few minutes more. Before the call ended, Corey urged her once more to give Brett a chance. Erin promised to think about it. She knew she really had no choice since it had been hard to think about anything else lately.

And then she took a deep breath and dialed Brett's number. Their conversation was rather strained that evening. Though they avoided the issue, they both knew that soon they'd have to talk about Brett's insistence on meeting. Claiming a headache, Erin brought the call to an early end. She spent a long time thinking that night, though she was no closer to a decision when she drifted to sleep than she'd been before. And her manufactured headache had become real.

THE NEW YORK BAR was trendy and crowded. Brett sat at a table with an associate from his publishing company, his favorite drink in front of him. And he was miserable.

"Hey, Brett. Check the babe in the corner. She's been giving you the eye, man."

In response to Jarrod's urgent murmur, Brett looked over his shoulder. The woman was tall, improbably auburn-haired, her stunningly curved figure displayed in minute detail by a skintight black lace minidress. And she was looking straight at him. She smiled, lifted an elegant eyebrow in obvious invitation, and leaned back against the bar as if waiting for him to join her.

There'd been a time when he'd have broken his neck to get to her. After all, he wasn't the type who usually had gorgeous women throwing passes at him. He was the one who'd generally done the passing before, beginning with an announcement of what he did for a living—something some women found interesting. He'd been reasonably successful with that strategy. It would probably work quite well with the woman who was looking at him now. He smiled at her, made a rueful gesture with his shoulders and turned back to his drink.

He wondered if Erin's hair was auburn. Or black, maybe? He wondered if she ever wore lace dresses and smiled at men in bars. She'd damn well better not be doing it tonight.

"I don't believe this," Jarrod muttered in blatant disgust. "She just moved on to someone else. You turned her down, man. Are you crazy?"

Brett shrugged. "Just not interested tonight."

"She's not a hooker or anything, you know. I know her—well, sort of. She's an advertising account exec. There are men who would maim and kill for an evening in her company."

"Guess I'm not one of them."

Jarrod scowled. "All right, who is she?"

"Which she?" Brett stalled.

"The woman who's got you wearing a Private Property sign. You're off the market, dude. Someone's put her brand on you."

Rolling his eyes at the cheerfully mixed metaphors, Brett shook his head. "You're the crazy one."

"Going to deny it, huh?"

"Deny what?" Brett asked blandly.

Jarrod, the best inker Brett had ever worked with, only scowled more fiercely. "Yeah, you're hooked. Got a ring through your nose and your heart on your sleeve. So, when's the wedding?"

Brett only laughed and changed the subject. *Wedding?* he thought wryly. There hadn't even been a meeting yet. He didn't expect his friend to understand that.

He wasn't even sure he understood it himself. He only knew that sometime during the past few days he'd come to a decision. No more sitting in an empty apartment, gazing longingly at the telephone. No more nights in bars, trying to work up interest in a woman who wasn't Erin. No more wondering what she looked like, who she was with when she wasn't talking to him, what it was that scared her so badly about meeting him.

He was going to find out for himself. He was leaving for Arkansas as soon as he had the chance to get back home and pack. He'd turned in a month's work that morning, so he had a few days available. He would use them getting to know Erin. Personally.

He glanced around the bar with a faint sense of smug satisfaction with his decision. Maybe he'd bring Erin here sometime. He'd like to do New York with her, after he'd shown her around Boston. There were a lot of things he wanted to do with her. Just the two of them. It would be great.

Now, all he had to do was convince her.

RUNNING A FINGER around the suddenly-too-tight collar of his pale blue shirt, Brett stared at the neat, unassuming home in front of him and wondered if he'd have the courage to ring the doorbell. What would Erin say when he introduced himself? he wondered for the thousandth time. Would she be furious with him for tracing her address through his reluctantly cooperative policeman brother-in-law? For showing up on her doorstep when she'd told him more than once that she wasn't ready to meet him?

Would she understand that he'd really had no other choice?

He took a deep breath. Courage had never been something he'd lacked. Some might even call it foolhardiness. He reached out to press the doorbell, listening in anticipation as it buzzed inside.

Forgive me, Erin. I waited as long as I could.

She wasn't at home. Of all the scenarios he'd imagined—that hadn't been one of them. Deflated, he sighed, ran a hand through his humidity-curled hair and looked around. What should he do now?

"She's probably at the park," a friendly voice called from the yard next door.

Looking around hopefully, Brett spotted the middle-aged woman working in an autumn-thinned flower bed. "I beg your pardon?"

"Erin always goes to the park on Saturday mornings. It's just three blocks that way." The woman pointed a green-gloved hand holding a dirty spade as she spoke.

Were Erin's neighbors always so talkative with strangers? Brett wondered in mild disapproval. The woman didn't know him, had no idea what his purpose was for ringing the bell, and yet she was cheerfully telling him where Erin could be found. And then he smiled. Why was he complaining? That was exactly what he'd wanted to know, wasn't it? "Thank you. I appreciate it."

The woman gave him a long, measuring look, then returned his smile with what almost looked like approval. "You're welcome."

He had no trouble finding a parking space for his rented car beside the park the woman had indicated. He discovered it to be a couple of acres of trees and picnic tables and playground equipment neatly situated in the centre of the middle-class neighborhood. It looked like a family sort of place. Brett wondered about that. He hadn't really expected Erin to live in a house, having thought she'd probably have an apartment or a condo. And why did she come to this park every Saturday morning?

Calling himself a fool for searching for a woman he wouldn't recognize anyway, he shoved his hands in the pockets of his navy slacks and wandered through the park. The place was crowded on this warm Saturday morning in mid-September. Children tumbled around him, squealing and squabbling, running toward the swings and slides and teeter-totters. Mothers of all shapes and sizes sat on benches, gossiping and keeping an eye on their younger kids. A few looked curiously at Brett, obviously unaccustomed to having strange men wander into their park.

He was just about to give up and leave when he saw the woman sitting alone on a redwood bench, reading a paperback book while she sipped at a canned cola. Her hair was dark, pinned loosely at the top of her head. Her face—a slightly squared oval, with delicate features—was enchanting, even behind the stylishly thin frames of the glasses she wore. Her pullover top clung attractively to full breasts, and a slender waist and khaki walking shorts made her golden legs seem to go on forever. She daintily licked a drop of soda from her full lower lip and his entire body tightened in response.

If this was Erin, he thought, he was a goner.

As if sensing him standing there staring at her, the woman looked up, her gaze meeting his. Her eyes were blue. Bright, vivid blue in delightful contrast to her dark hair. He had a sudden urge to see himself reflected in them. "Hi," he managed, gesturing awkwardly to the empty half of the bench on which she sat. "Mind if I sit down?"

She scooted closer to her end. "No, of course not. It's a public bench, after all."

Erin. He'd know her voice anywhere. Exhaling sound-lessly, he sat down, still staring at her. So now he had a face to go with the voice. A beautiful, compelling face to match a bright, clever mind.

He felt the smile spread across his face as he slipped painlessly, hopelessly into love.

6

ERIN FELT HER CHEEKS warm beneath the man's intense inspection. She'd had other men stare at her, of course, attracted by whatever it was men found so appealing about her. But, for some reason, this one was different. There was something in his smiling, golden-brown eyes that she couldn't quite analyze.

She took a moment to study him in response before turning back to her book. He looked young, probably only a year or two older than her own twenty-six. His hair was brown, thick and curly, glinting with reddish highlights in the morning sun. His nose was appealingly crooked. His cheeks were square, slashed by disarming dimples. He was slim and fit, though not particularly tall. He looked nice. She couldn't help returning his smile.

As if encouraged by her reaction, he shifted to half face her. "Beautiful day, isn't it?"

"Yes, very nice," she agreed, amused by the bland, predictable opening line. At least he hadn't come out with something that sounded as if it belonged in a tacky singles-bar setting. She'd heard all of those already. They'd never worked for her.

"What's your name?"

He watched her face as he asked the question, as if hoping he hadn't become too personal, too quickly. She rather liked his diffidence. His uncertainty made her feel less wary than she might have been, had he come on too strong. "Erin," she supplied, not bothering with the surname.

"Erin. What a beautiful name," he murmured.

It sounded like something Brett would have said. In fact, this man could fit the mental picture she'd drawn of Brett during the past few months. But Brett was in Boston. This man's voice wasn't as deep and carried no trace of the Eastern accent that occasionally crept into Brett's. And she couldn't imagine Brett's smile edged with just the hint of shyness she found so appealing in this man. After all, why would Brett be shy with her? "Thank you," she said, then turned back to her book for lack of anything else to say.

She looked up when he cleared his throat.

"Uh—you come here often?" he asked, then winced. "Sorry. That was pretty lame, wasn't it? I might as well have asked your sign."

Disarmed by his self-deprecating smile, she laughed at his lapse into the singles-bar chatter she'd thought about only minutes before. "Actually, I do come here often. And I'm a Libra. What about you?"

He chuckled. "Sagittarius. Maybe I'd better go back to talking about the weather. Think it's going to get hot this afternoon?"

Intrigued, Erin closed her book, holding her place with one finger. "Yes, very. It's supposed to rain tomorrow, I hear."

Grinning broadly, the man nodded. "So they say. How's your book?"

"Interesting." She showed him the cover of the recent paperback bestseller, a romantic suspense by Nora Roberts, one of her favorite writers.

He glanced at it, then nodded. "I've read that. It's very good. Want to know who the murderer is?"

"No, not yet, thanks," she answered in amusement. "I'm surprised you read it. Her readers are usually women."

"A friend recommended it," he replied. "I think good writing appeals to everyone, don't you?"

She smiled. "It certainly should. Have you read any of her other books?"

"One. *Sacred Sins*."

"Oh, I loved that one! Did you know who the killer was? She had me completely stumped. I was so surprised by the ending."

They spent the next ten minutes discussing that book and several others they'd both read and enjoyed. Erin was surprised at how easily she and this attractive stranger conversed. She didn't generally talk so readily to strangers, particularly men. But it was nice to sit in a park, chatting with a man who regarded her with appreciation, a man with delightful manners and a touch of old-fashioned courtesy that appealed to her.

She couldn't help thinking of Brett. It was easy to talk to him, of course. But she wasn't sure it would be this easy if she agreed to meet him in person. After all, she'd told him things she'd never told anyone else. Their conversations had been almost embarrassingly frank at times. She wasn't sure she'd be able to look at him without blushing in recollection.

This man, on the other hand, knew nothing about her except her name and her taste in books, which made everything much less awkward. Nothing personal at all. Including, it seemed, the fact that she had a daughter. He looked stunned when Chelsea ran up to the bench to ask Erin to tie her shoe.

Studying him out of the corner of her eye, Erin bent to the tiny Reebok sneaker, wondering why he looked so surprised. Hadn't he known she was here with her child?

She'd half assumed he had one running around somewhere. That was usually why adults found themselves in this park. If not that, why was he here?

Why hadn't she told him? Brett stared at the dark-haired little girl in dismay. She'd called Erin "Mommy." Not that the words had been necessary. The child was a miniature duplicate of her mother, with the same dark hair and almost-oval face. Only the eyes were different; the child's were dark, almost black—the dark, mysterious, slightly uptilted eyes of a future heartbreaker. "This is your—uh—?"

"My daughter," Erin supplied, straightening from her task. "Chelsea. Chels, this is Mr.—?"

"Hi, Chelsea," Brett said, smiling at the child as he deliberately ignored Erin's implied question. "It's very nice to meet you."

The little girl looked him over gravely, glancing at her mother to make sure it was all right to talk to the man. When Erin nodded permission, Chelsea turned to Brett with a smile that captivated him. "I'm going to be four after Thanksgiving. I'm getting a training bike for my birthday."

"Are you? Can you ride?"

"Not yet, but Mommy's going to teach me. Aren't you, Mommy?"

"Of course I am," Erin assured her. "But that's still a couple of months away, sweetie."

"I know." Chelsea sighed. "I have a dance recital next month," she announced. "I have a red-and-white costume and I get to wear a feather in my hair."

"I'm sure you'll look beautiful," Brett replied. "Do you like to dance?"

"Mm-hmm. I like tap better than ballet, though. Ballet's boring. Can I go slide, Mommy?"

"May I," Erin corrected automatically. "Yes, but be careful."

"Okay. Bye," she added to Brett, just before turning and dashing away, her ponytail swinging over her hot-pink-and-white playsuit.

Why hadn't she told him she had a daughter? Brett looked at Erin, hurt and even irritated by the omission. She'd told him so much about herself. Hadn't she considered a child a rather important part of her life?

A recently recurring fantasy replayed in his mind. Walking hand in hand in the Common on a beautiful, fragrant autumn day, the sounds of sidewalk performers and laughing conversations tangling in the air. Just Brett and Erin . . . and her three-year-old daughter. Somehow it just wasn't the same now.

"So you have a daughter," he said and his voice sounded a bit hollow even to him. "Any other kids?"

She shook her head, to his relief. "Just Chelsea. What about you? Are you here with children?"

"No, I don't have any kids. I was just—uh—" He hated lying to her, still wasn't even sure why he hadn't yet told her who he was. He decided to blame that on Cheryl. "Just strolling through the park enjoying the nice weather," he finished lamely.

Great, he thought with a mental groan. Back to the weather again. Chelsea's arrival had really knocked him for a loop.

It wasn't that he had anything against children, he reflected. It was just that he'd never lusted over anyone's mother before.

What should he do now? he asked himself, frantically trying to think of something to say. Should he tell her the truth? If he did, would she snatch up her daughter and storm away? Would she turn distant and awkward, suspicious of his sudden appearance? He ruefully suspected she wouldn't throw herself into his arms and welcome him to her town.

Dammit, Cheryl. What have you gotten me into now?

During his silence, Erin had turned back to her book, though he knew she was still aware of him. He cleared his throat. "Your daughter looks very much like you. Except for her eyes, of course. She—uh—has your husband's eyes?"

"My ex-husband's," Erin corrected.

"Oh." He looked at his hands, then at her. This wasn't going to work, he decided abruptly. He couldn't go on deceiving her about who he was, couldn't ask her out without telling the truth. "Erin, I—"

"Mo-o-mmy." Sobbing, Chelsea interrupted them, holding up two dirty hands as she approached them, both knees covered with dirt. "I fell down. My hands are bleeding."

Brett almost cringed at the sight of bright red drops of blood oozing from the tiny scraped palms. Erin didn't seem particularly disturbed as she took Chelsea's hands in hers. "Yes, I see they are," she said bracingly. "We'll go home and put some antiseptic on them."

Chelsea's lip quivered. "Will it hurt?"

"No, of course not. Remember the new brand we found that doesn't sting a bit?"

The child nodded. "Can I have orange pop?"

"Yes, with your lunch, after we clean your hands."

Tears already drying, Chelsea pressed her advantage a bit more. "And ice cream?"

Erin smiled ruefully at Brett. "Children become masters of manipulation at a very early age," she murmured before turning back to Chelsea. "We'll talk about it when we get home."

She tucked her book under her arm and stood. Suddenly realizing that she was leaving, Brett rose quickly to his feet. Erin turned to look at him and he realized that she had an inch advantage in height. He wondered glumly how she felt about guys who were shorter than she was. And then he wondered when he was ever going to have the chance to find out. "Erin, I—"

"Hurry, Mommy. My hands are still bleeding," Chelsea whined restlessly, fanning her stinging palms in the air. "They need 'septic."

"Yes, I'm coming, Chelsea." Erin looked apologetically at Brett. "It was nice to meet you."

He just managed not to wince. "Yeah. You, too," he muttered, conceding defeat this time. "Maybe we'll see each other again sometime."

"Maybe," she agreed, and he could tell by her expression that she didn't believe they would. "Goodbye."

He didn't repeat the goodbye. Unlike Erin, he knew they'd be seeing each other again. Soon. God help him.

CHERYL WAS PRACTICALLY waiting for him at her front door when he returned. "Well," she demanded, hardly giving him time to get inside. "Did you meet her? What's she like? Was she mad that you looked her up? Is she beautiful?"

Brett held up both hands. "Slow down, Cheryl. One question at a time, okay? And would you mind if I have a drink while you interrogate me?"

"There are cold colas in the refrigerator. Help yourself."

"Thanks." He walked past her into the kitchen. She followed right on his heels. "Where are the boys?" he asked, noticing the house was unusually peaceful. His nephews, ages five and four, were rarely still or quiet.

"Taking their naps," Cheryl explained with a sigh of relief. "It's always a hassle to get them down, but so wonderful while it lasts. We've got another hour of respite. So tell me about Erin. Did you meet her?"

"I met her," Brett answered, swinging a leg over one of the straight-backed chairs at the kitchen table and setting the canned cola in front of him. "Sort of."

"Have you had lunch? You want a sandwich or something? And what do you mean, 'Sort of'?"

Used to his sister's habit of carrying on at least two conversations at once, Brett only shrugged. "Yeah, a sandwich sounds good, if you don't mind."

She rummaged in the refrigerator. "What do you mean, sort of?" she repeated, obviously intent on learning every detail.

"I found her in a park close to her house. We talked a few minutes. I—uh—didn't tell her who I was."

Spreading mayonnaise on whole-wheat bread, Cheryl looked over her shoulder. "Why not?"

He shrugged. "Your fault. I guess I thought I was meeting her incognito."

She giggled. "Chicken."

"Yeah. When the time came to say my name, I couldn't do it. I thought I'd give her a chance to find out what a really nice, harmless—well, relatively harmless—guy I am, and then I'd confess the truth."

"It's a great plan," Cheryl assured him. "After all, it *was* my idea. So, did it work?"

"We got interrupted before I could make much headway."

"By what?" she asked, sliding a loaded plate in front of him.

"Her daughter." Brett picked up the thick sandwich she'd made. "She's got a three-year-old kid. She never told me."

"Oh." Cheryl waited until he'd taken a bite before asking, "Does that make a difference to you?"

Brett swallowed, trying to decide how to answer. "I'm not sure," he said finally.

"Well, why not? It shouldn't matter that she has a daughter."

"What matters," Brett muttered, "is that she didn't tell me. I can't help wondering what else she kept from me during the past few months."

"I see." Cheryl thought about it for the next few minutes while he ate, then asked carefully, "Could her daughter be the reason she was so wary about meeting you? You didn't give her any reason to believe you don't like kids, did you?"

Brett thought back to a conversation he and Erin had had not long after they'd started talking.

Do you like children? she'd asked.

Sure, he'd answered. *From a distance.*

He shifted uncomfortably in the chair. "Uh—well, maybe. I mean, she may have misinterpreted something I once said."

Cheryl rolled her eyes in disgust. "Men!" she muttered.

Was Cheryl right about Erin's reasons for putting him off? He sighed, finally understanding her hesitation. After all, she had a child to think of. She had more than herself to consider.

The question was, did he want to become involved with a woman with the responsibilities inherent in raising a child?

Did he really have any choice?

As if reading her brother's mind, Cheryl questioned, "*Does* it make a difference, Brett? Are you going to see her again?"

"Yeah," he said quietly. "I'm going to see her again."

"So, you're not mad at her anymore for not telling you about her daughter?"

"I guess I understand why she didn't," Brett conceded, though he still wanted to hear Erin's explanation.

"And you don't mind that she has a child?"

He shrugged. "I guess not. I mean, why should it? She seemed like a nice kid. And there are always baby-sitters."

Cheryl looked concerned. "There's a bit more to it than that," she murmured. "Children aren't a minor inconvenience you have to work around, Brett."

"I know," he replied defensively. "Just—let me take it one step at a time, okay?"

Cheryl leaned against the table across from him, resting her chin on her fists. "So, how did you find her in the park? How did you recognize her?"

Brett chuckled, shaking his head. "You probably won't believe this, but I walked straight to her. And as soon as I heard her talk, I knew I'd guessed correctly."

"Wow. It must be fate," Cheryl mused, her brown eyes going dreamy.

"Maybe it is," Brett agreed, remembering the almost-physical impact Erin's beautiful blue eyes had had upon him. "Maybe it is."

ERIN WAS THINKING about the man from the park as she cleaned the kitchen that evening. Chelsea was tucked into bed and the house was quiet except for the radio playing from the kitchen counter. *A very nice man*, she found herself thinking again. *Attractive, too, in a wholesome, guy-next-door way*. It was the first time a man had appealed to her in that way in quite some time. She'd sensed that the attraction was mutual. In fact, if Chelsea hadn't interrupted when she had, Erin thought he might have asked her out.

What would she have said if he had? After all, he was a total stranger. Yet she realized in some surprise that she would have been tempted to say yes. Very tempted. It had been so long since she'd been on a date, since she'd eaten in a restaurant where the food wasn't served on carry-yourself trays by people with clowns on their ID badges. Hadn't she been telling herself she needed to get out more? Hadn't Adam insinuated that the reason she was so fascinated by her telephone friend was because she was sublimating her natural need to spend more time with adults—in particular, male adults?

Would a more active social life help her sleep better? Make her stop tossing and turning and dreaming of a fantasy lover who was no more in reality than a voice on the telephone?

And why, dammit, was she suddenly feeling guilty for considering going out with a man she'd met in the park, a man she'd probably never see again? What was this misguided sense of loyalty to Brett? She'd told him she didn't want to meet him. If only she could make herself believe it.

As if her thoughts of Brett had prompted it, the telephone rang. Erin stared at it for a moment before picking it up, again plagued by a nagging sense of disloyalty. Then, telling herself she was being an idiot, she picked up the receiver. "Hello."

"Hi, Erin."

The deep voice went straight to her knees. She sank into a chair at the kitchen table. "Hi, Brett."

"How are you?"

"I'm okay," she returned vaguely. "How about you?"

He sighed through the line. "I'm getting damned frustrated."

She winced, knowing what was coming next. She was right.

"I want to see you, Erin."

"Brett, don't start this again."

"I'm not going to stop. It's getting ridiculous. You're important to me. You're a part of my life. I want to see you."

"Brett, I—"

He broke in with a new note in his voice that she hadn't heard before—a firm, no-nonsense, very male note that made a shiver of awareness course down her spine. "All right, Erin, let's have it. What, exactly, is holding you back? What aren't you telling me?"

She widened her eyes, thinking immediately of Chelsea. Should she tell him? If so, what words could she use to explain that she was afraid her relationship with Brett could only end up hurting her daughter? How could she make him understand that Chelsea came first, would always come first with her? "What makes you think there's something I'm not telling you?" she countered.

"I've gotten to know you pretty well during the past few months. I know the way you sound when you're not being entirely honest with me. What is it, Erin? Was your relationship with Martin so horrible that you can never trust another man?"

"That's part of it," she admitted candidly. "Martin changed me, Brett. I went into our relationship naive and optimistic and hopelessly romantic. I came out hurt and bitter and with very few illusions left. It's taken me a long time to get over the anger and the pain. I don't want to go through that again."

"What makes you think we'd end up like you and your jerk of an ex-husband?" he demanded. "There's no comparison. Martin wanted you for your youth, your beauty. I'm interested in your mind, your opinions, your wonderful sense of humor. We have so much in common, Erin. So much more going for us than most couples just starting out in a relationship. Why are you so sure we're doomed to failure? What do I have to do to convince you I'm not like him?"

"I've never said you were like Martin," Erin answered defensively.

"You've implied it. And yet I've just told you that I'm not particularly concerned with appearances. I'm not worried about growing older, the way he was. Actually, I'm looking forward to a few interesting lines and gray hairs," he added, striving for a lighter note. "Maybe they'll help me get away from the 'cute' look and take on a more distinguished air."

"Maybe they will," Erin agreed.

"I don't wear gold chains and I'd never pull my hair back into a little ponytail. I don't carve notches into my bedpost. How did Martin feel about kids and animals?" he asked deliberately, still in that teasing vein but oddly serious with the question.

"He—uh—" She cleared her throat. "He didn't like either of them. Never wanted either a pet or—or a child."

"Well, there you go. Something else different about the two of us. I happen to like pets. And children."

"From a distance," she reminded him faintly.

"I was only teasing when I said that. Really. I like kids."

She couldn't help but be suspicious about his sudden preoccupation with that particular topic. It was almost as if he knew about . . . But he couldn't, she reminded herself. How could he have found out about Chelsea? She remained silent, not quite knowing what to say.

"Erin, what would you do if I suddenly showed up on your doorstep? Would you close the door in my face, refuse to talk to me?"

"I don't know," she whispered, having asked herself that same question more than once. "But you don't know where I live, so I don't suppose I have to worry about that, do I?"

He hesitated. "I just want to know what you'd do," he insisted without answering her question.

Erin wearily pushed a strand of hair out of her face. "You're giving me a headache," she accused him, rubbing at her temple with her free hand. "Why don't you give me time to think about what you've said tonight?"

"How much time?"

"I don't know," she murmured again. "I just . . . need to think, Brett. About a lot of things."

"Well, think fast, Erin. I want to see you. Dammit, I need to see you. And I don't know how much longer I can wait."

"You're pushing me."

"Yes," he admitted without hesitation. "I know I am. But I can't help it. Don't you see that I really have no other choice?"

Maybe he was right, she thought despondently. Maybe neither of them would ever be able to go on with their normal lives until they'd gotten the meeting out of the way. But she couldn't quite work up the nerve to agree yet. She needed more time. "I'll think about it," she promised again.

"You do that," he suggested. "I'll talk to you soon, Erin."

"All right. Good night, Brett."

"Good night, Erin."

She hung up with the sense that control of this unusual relationship was about to be taken out of her hands. If it hadn't been already.

THAT NIGHT Erin dreamed, as she had before, that she and Brett were making love. His deep, so-familiar voice murmured words of love and appreciation into her ears as he caressed her. Only this time he had a face to go with the voice. Oddly enough, she'd given him the face of the man she'd met in the park.

She woke with a start, blinking at the morning light pouring through the bedroom window. What a strange dream! She got out of bed and headed for the kitchen. She needed coffee.

She was still thinking about the dream, still puzzling over its meaning, when a familiar tap on the back door made her cross the kitchen and pull the door open. "Good morning, Isabelle. I just made coffee. Would you like a cup?"

Her neighbor shook her gray head with a smile. "No, thanks, dear, I have to get ready for church. But I had these fresh blackberry muffins left over from breakfast and I thought you and Chelsea might like them this morning."

Erin took the basket gratefully. "They smell heavenly. Thank you."

"By the way, did that attractive young man find you yesterday?"

Surprised by the question, Erin looked curiously at Isabelle. "What attractive young man?"

"The one who came calling while you were at the park yesterday morning. I normally wouldn't have told just anyone where you were, but he looked so nice. He reminded me of my nephew, Andrew. Curly brown hair, lovely smile. And very courteous. A new suitor?" she asked hopefully.

Curly brown hair. Lovely smile.

What would you do if I suddenly showed up on your doorstep? Brett had asked. But Brett was in Boston. He'd called from there only the night before. Hadn't he?

Of course, he'd never actually said he was still in Boston. She'd only assumed . . .

"You said you told him I was at the park?" she asked Isabelle slowly.

Beginning to look concerned at whatever she read in Erin's face, the older woman nodded. "Yes. I hope I did the right thing. Maybe I shouldn't have . . . ?"

"No, it's all right, Isabelle," Erin assured her quickly, not wanting her friend to worry.

Isabelle didn't look convinced. "Maybe I shouldn't do that again?"

"Maybe not," Erin agreed gently. "But, really, don't worry about it. This time it was a friend." *Or, rather, an ex-friend.*

She was an idiot, she told herself as she closed the door behind her neighbor. A full-fledged, gullible idiot for falling for his clever smile and skillful evasions.

He'd deceived her.

She must have known all along, subconsciously. That's why she'd had the dream, she reflected, growing angrier with every passing minute. And that's why he'd looked so stunned when he'd found out about Chelsea. He had known where to find Erin, but he hadn't known she had a child.

Her cheeks flaming, she paced the kitchen, her steps short, crisp, forceful. Snatches of frank, intimate, sometimes risqué conversation ran through her mind. Why had she talked so candidly to him, secure in the misguided belief that they'd never meet? She should have known better than to play games that had no rules. She should have listened to Adam.

How had Brett found her? That was one of the questions she intended to ask him, just before she told him exactly what she thought of him for deceiving her. She didn't doubt that he'd be back. Soon. Probably today.

When he came, she'd be ready for him. *The rat*.

Turning toward her bedroom, she decided to get ready, not wanting to be caught off guard. She'd practice her speech to him in the shower. She wanted to make her displeasure perfectly clear when she talked to him.

He was the one who'd wanted honesty. Who'd insisted on a face-to-face meeting. Fine. That's exactly what she'd give him.

7

BRETT PULLED HIS RENTAL car into Erin's drive, determined to get the confrontation behind him. He'd waited until early afternoon, but he couldn't wait any longer. He'd been wrong to deceive her, wrong not to tell her who he was in the park yesterday. Now it was time to confess and then try to salvage something from the resulting explosion.

Now that he'd actually seen her, he was even more obsessed with her than he'd been before. He'd spent most of the night adjusting to his new knowledge about her: the fact that she had a child. He'd decided it didn't matter. He wanted Erin. If she came as a package deal, fine. He'd take her any way he could get her.

If only he could convince Erin to forgive him—for the deception, and for forcing a meeting she'd resisted.

He rang the doorbell with a not-quite-steady finger. The door was thrown open more quickly than he'd expected, catching him off guard. Almost as if she'd been waiting for him. Something in her eyes made him catch his breath.

She knows, he thought, startled. *How could she possibly know?*

"Hello, Erin," he said quietly, studying the fiery glitter in her vivid blue eyes with wary interest. She wasn't wearing the glasses this time, he noted automatically.

She tilted her head in obviously feigned surprise, her dark hair swaying at her shoulders. She wore jeans and a rather militarily styled black shirt that only enhanced the femininity of her delicate features. His body tightened in fierce response; the desire he'd felt the day before was only strengthened by seeing her again.

"Why, it's the man from the park," she murmured, her voice much too smooth.

"Well—um—"

"Please, come in." She stepped aside, waving an invitation with one slender hand.

Since she didn't even ask how he'd found her or what he was doing there, Brett was even more positive that she already knew who he was. He stepped carefully past her, looking around for her daughter. "Where's Chelsea?"

"She's making chocolate-chip cookies with our neighbor, Mrs. Price. You should remember her—she's the one who gave you directions to the park yesterday."

Brett winced. So that was how she'd figured it out.

"So, tell me, stranger," she continued, planting her hands on her slender hips and looking him straight in the eye, "what can I do for you? Are you, perhaps, selling insurance? Encyclopedias?"

"Erin—"

She cocked her head. "No? Then perhaps you're a reporter, looking for a story. Something having to do with a woman you assume to be a naive idiot."

"I don't think you're a naive idiot," Brett said wearily. This was going to be worse than he'd expected.

"How would you know? After all, we just met yesterday, didn't we, *stranger?*"

"That's enough, Erin. You obviously know who I am."

"All I know is what you told me yesterday, remember?"

His own temper was beginning to ignite, despite his awareness that he deserved her anger. Perhaps *because* of that awareness. "I said that's enough, Erin. We need to talk and we can't do that as long as you're taking potshots at me."

Her eyes widened, her cheeks darkened with emotion. "You have the *nerve* to criticize me for being furious with you? *You lied to me!*"

"I didn't—" He stopped with a sigh. "Yeah, I guess I did, in a way. I'm sorry."

She wasn't appeased. "That's supposed to be enough?"

"It's the best I can do," he answered evenly. "I *am* sorry, Erin. I wanted a few minutes to talk to you without scaring you off or making you self-conscious. And I enjoyed talking with you for those few minutes. I would have told you the truth if we hadn't been interrupted. I knew I couldn't deceive you for long."

"You shouldn't have deceived me at all," she snapped, arms crossing defensively at her waist. "You should have told me who you were from the beginning. Or at least you should have said something during that call last night. Dammit, you shouldn't have even been there in the first place! You agreed to give me time."

He narrowed his eyes, clenching his fists in his tight jeans pockets. "I think I've groveled just about enough," he informed her in clipped words. "Okay, so what I did was wrong. But I'm not the only one who hasn't been exactly honest, am I? At least I only deceived you for a few minutes. You've been lying to me for nearly four months!"

Stung, she lifted her chin defiantly. "I have *not* been lying to you!"

He crossed his own arms, tucking his hands into the crooks of his elbows to keep them from reaching out for her. Even furious, she was the most striking woman he'd ever seen. He couldn't remember ever wanting anyone like this. The wanting was a hunger gnawing voraciously inside him, making it hard for him to think clearly, hard to control his volatile emotions.

"I suppose you simply forgot to mention that you had a three-year-old daughter?" he said sarcastically.

Her cheeks flamed. "No, I didn't forget," she muttered. "I didn't think it was any of your business!"

He felt as if she'd slugged him. "None of my business?" he repeated incredulously, staring at her.

She shifted uncomfortably on her feet, not quite meeting his eyes. "It's just that we—that I—"

He didn't allow her to finish whatever she'd tried to say. Catching her forearms in his hands, he barely resisted the impulse to shake her. Eye to eye, toe to toe, he faced her, speaking in a low, clear, furious voice. "I've told you things I've never told anyone. Things no one else could possibly understand. But *you* did—or at least, I thought you did. I thought we had something special. If nothing else, I thought we were friends. And you didn't think it was my business that you have a child?"

"Brett," she whispered, "I—"

"Tell me, Erin, do your other friends know about Chelsea? Do you make it a regular habit to conceal her existence?"

"No, of course not. All my friends know about her. But—"

"All your *real* friends, you mean," he cut in bitterly. "Just how did I fit into your life, Erin? If not a friend, what was I to you?"

She tossed her head in agitation, her dark hair flying around her face. "You were a fantasy! An escape. Someone with whom I could pretend, just for a few precious hours, that I was more than Chelsea's mom. Someone to talk to and laugh with and share witty repartee and inside jokes. Someone—the only one, I thought—who didn't expect anything from me, didn't care about my responsibilities or obligations."

He deliberately eased his hold on her, his fingers caressing rather than binding. "That wasn't a fantasy," he murmured huskily. "I don't care about those things. And I know you're more than Chelsea's mom. You're Erin."

Her eyes sad, she shook her head slowly. "You still don't understand. I *am* Chelsea's mom. First and foremost. I'm not free to jump into impulsive relationships or become involved with any man who catches my interest. What I do affects her. The men I date become a part of her life, as well. Men look at me and they see—I don't know—someone different from who I really am. Someone suitable for fun and games and free-spirited affairs. Well, I can't be that person. I have Chelsea."

Genuinely confused, he tried to understand. "You didn't want to meet me because you thought I wouldn't understand about your daughter? Because you thought I'd try to separate you from her?"

"You wouldn't be the first," she replied in little more than a whisper. "And you can't convince me that you were overjoyed to find out about her. I saw your face when she ran up to the park bench yesterday. I didn't understand why you looked so stunned then. Now I do."

"Yeah, I was stunned," he agreed dryly. "How could I not have been? I had no idea you had a child. And, I have to admit, it took me a little while to adapt to this new image of you. But it hasn't changed anything, Erin. I still think we're special together. That we have a better foundation for a relationship than most couples who have dated for months. That we'd be crazy to give up on it without even trying to see where it leads."

"And if it leads nowhere?" she asked tightly, her hands lifting to rest on his chest as she searched his face.

"Isn't that a risk everyone has to take sometime?"

"I don't want Chelsea hurt," she insisted stubbornly.

"I'm not going to hurt your daughter, Erin. Or you. Give me a chance to prove it, will you?"

She looked at him suspiciously. "How?"

The urge to shake her returned—not as strongly this time, but he was still exasperated. "How does anyone find out more about someone? Go out with me. Have dinner, talk—you know, date? Don't you think it's past time we had a first date?"

She frowned suddenly. "How did you find me, anyway?"

"My brother-in-law's with the NLRPD," he answered. "And, yeah, he shouldn't have looked you up for me, so I hope you won't turn him in. He owed me a couple of favors. Will you have dinner with me tonight, Erin?"

She gnawed on her lower lip while she thought about her answer. The unconsciously seductive act was almost his undoing. He wanted to kiss her so badly he ached with it; wanted to taste her, to imprint himself on her so she'd stop fighting the inevitable. He'd been wanting her for months—even before he'd ever set eyes on her. Now that he had, the wanting was almost more than he could take.

"Erin?" he demanded hoarsely.

She released her lip, moistening it with the tip of her tongue. He almost groaned. "All right, Brett," she murmured. "I'll have dinner with you tonight. I'll see if I can find a baby-sitter for Chelsea."

"You don't have to do that," he said, remembering that she worried about him not wanting to have anything to do with her daughter. Though he'd rather have Erin to himself, at least this first time, he wanted even more for her to know that he could deal with her responsibilities to her kid. "Bring her along. We'll have burgers or pizza or something, and get to know each other."

She shook her head, with an expression that was hard to read. "No. I think it will be better if she stays with a baby-sitter this time."

"You do whatever you think best."

"When it comes to Chelsea, I always do," she answered immediately.

It was impossible to continue standing so close to her without wanting to be closer. His fingers tightening on her arms, he drew her an inch nearer. "I know you don't want to hear this, Erin, but you really are beautiful. More beautiful than I'd ever imagined."

"I never said I didn't want to hear compliments," she responded with a half smile. "I'm as vain as any other woman."

Compared to some of the women he knew, there wasn't a vain bone in Erin's body. He didn't bother to tell her so. Instead, he smiled and pulled her even closer, so that her full breasts just brushed his chest. Her lips were only inches from his. She moistened them again, nervously, but didn't draw away. Her gaze locked with his and he saw curiosity there, as well as sensuality.

She wanted him to kiss her, he thought exultantly.

She wanted him to kiss her, she realized in dismay.

Reading the intent in his eyes, Erin swallowed and tried desperately to think clearly. She was still angry with him—wasn't she? Still furious, even hurt, that he'd deceived her, that he'd ignored her requests to give her time to decide whether she wanted to meet him. She tried to focus on those negative feelings. Instead, she could only think of how very much she wanted him to kiss her.

"You shouldn't have come here," she whispered—a weak reminder to him—and to herself—that there were still many problems standing between them.

He lifted a hand, sliding his fingers into her hair as his palm cradled her cheek. "Are you really sorry I did?" he asked, looking at her with a mixture of challenge and entreaty.

"I—" Was she? At the moment, she honestly couldn't have said. "I don't know," she answered candidly.

The silence lingered. His hand was so warm against her face, tempting her to snuggle more deeply into the light embrace. How long had it been since anyone had touched her so tenderly? Why hadn't she realized how much she'd craved that tenderness?

His thumb slid slowly over her lower lip. "Erin," he murmured, somehow making her name a caress.

She trembled. "Brett, I—I'm not a spontaneous, impulsive person," she managed, her voice strained with emotion. "I need time. I have responsibilities . . ."

His hand slid to the back of her head as his mouth covered hers.

Erin closed her eyes and melted into him, forgetting responsibilities, forgetting everything except the longings that had been building inside her with each intimate telephone conversation they'd had. Longings to be held, to be kissed, to be wanted by the man who'd laughed with her and talked with her and listened to her so many times; who'd brought excitement and fantasy and desire back into her life after the long years of duty and self-denial. He wasn't a stranger, wasn't a man she'd met only the day before. He was Brett, and she'd been dreaming of his kisses for months.

The kiss was thorough, yet gentle, making her feel pampered and cherished and so very special—feelings she

GET 4 BOOKS

FREE

Return this card, and we'll send you 4 brand-new Harlequin Temptation® novels, absolutely *FREE!* We'll even pay the postage both ways!

We're making you this offer to introduce you to the benefits of the Harlequin Reader Service®: free home delivery of brand-new romance novels, **AND** at a saving of 30¢ apiece compared to the cover price!

Accepting these 4 free books places you under no obligation to continue. You may cancel at any time, even just after receiving your free shipment. If you do not cancel, every month, we'll send 4 more Harlequin Temptation® novels and bill you just $2.69* apiece—that's all!

Yes! Please send me my 4 free Harlequin Temptation® novels, as explained above.

Name

Address   Apt.

City   State   Zip

142 CIH ADGT (U-H-T-11/91)

Get 4 Books FREE

SEE BACK OF CARD FOR DETAILS

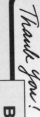

FREE MYSTERY GIFT

We will be happy to send you a free bonus gift. To request it, please check here, and mail this reply card promptly!

Thank you!

BUSINESS REPLY CARD

FIRST CLASS MAIL   PERMIT NO. 717   BUFFALO, NY

POSTAGE WILL BE PAID BY ADDRESSEE

HARLEQUIN READER SERVICE®

3010 WALDEN AVE
P O BOX 1867
BUFFALO NY 14240-9952

DETACH ALONG DOTTED LINE AND MAIL TODAY! – DETACH ALONG DOTTED LINE AND MAIL TODAY! – DETACH ALONG DOTTED LINE AND MAIL TODAY! – DETACH ALONG DOTTED LINE AND MAIL TODAY!

hadn't had in years, if ever. Her willpower dissolved. Her arms slid around his neck and she strained closer to him, losing herself in the pleasure he gave her.

Brett pulled his mouth away slowly, tightening his arms around her. His eyes mirrored the same dazed awe she felt. "Erin," he murmured hoarsely, "I've wanted you for so long. You couldn't possibly know how much I've wanted you."

Couldn't she? She brought her mouth back to his to show him differently. He groaned his approval, his tongue sweeping past her parted lips to tangle eagerly with hers.

Participating wholeheartedly in the kiss, Erin wondered at how beautifully they fit together. Martin stood well over six feet, as had most of the other men she'd dated, making her feel small and, at times, vulnerable. With Brett she was an equal. Their mouths met effortlessly. Her breasts pressed tightly against his solid chest. Their thighs brushed and hers cradled his straining manhood. It took very little effort to imagine them together in bed, tangled in perfect alignment. The erotic images made her moan into his mouth.

Responding to that sensual sound, Brett pulled her even closer, sliding one hand to the small of her back to mold her against his bold need. "Erin, I—"

"Mommy?"

The child's voice broke into the sensual haze surrounding them. Erin pulled out of Brett's arms with a gasp, turning to find her daughter standing in the kitchen doorway, a basket clutched in her tiny hands. "Chelsea." She cleared her throat, automatically straightening her hair. "Did you finish making cookies with Mrs. Price?"

"They're all done. She gave me some to bring home." Chelsea stared at Brett. "Why were you hugging my mommy?"

"Because I like her," Brett replied easily, dropping to one knee to bring himself on a level with the child. "Don't you hug people you like?"

Chelsea nodded, dark braid bobbing. "I hugged Mrs. Price when I left. I like her a lot."

"There, you see? Boy, those cookies smell good."

Chelsea smiled in shy pleasure that made Erin wary. There were so few men in Chelsea's life. Erin was particularly concerned that Chelsea would become attached to Brett before any of them knew where this relationship would lead. She would simply have to take steps to make sure that didn't happen, she told herself firmly.

"You were at the park yesterday," Chelsea informed Brett, cocking her head in recognition.

"Yes," he confirmed. "My name is Brett."

"I think we'd better make it Mr. Nash," Erin corrected quickly.

Brett only looked over his shoulder at her. "Mr. Nash is my father. I'm Brett."

Chelsea looked from the man kneeling in front of her to her mother, visibly confused. Reading the determination in Brett's steady gaze, Erin relented rather than cause an awkward scene. "All right. Brett."

Chelsea smiled. "I like that name," she told him.

Brett returned the grin, reaching out to tug lightly on the child's braid. "I like your name, too."

"You want a cookie? I put the chocolate chips in by myself. I only had one so I could eat more with Mommy, but it was really good," she assured him earnestly.

"I'd love to have a cookie. Thank you."

Chelsea was already digging into the basket. Sighing, Erin stepped forward. "Let's take them into the kitchen and I'll pour everyone a glass of milk to go with them. And then Brett has to go," she added with a meaningful look at him. "I have some things to do before tonight."

Brett only smiled. She knew he'd contented himself with his victory in talking her into having dinner with him that evening. She still wasn't exactly sure how he'd done it, but she needed time alone before they left for that date. Time to think about what had just happened. To decide whether she wanted it to happen again. As if she had any choice in the matter. She knew that Brett would only have to touch her to have her falling into his arms again.

She definitely had a lot to think about before dinner that evening.

ERIN GAZED ACROSS the linen-covered table at Brett. Why had they been able to talk so easily over the telephone as strangers when they were having such trouble making conversation tonight?

Pleating her napkin in her lap, she tried to think of something to say to break the tense silence. Nothing came immediately to mind. She moistened her lips and looked to Brett for help.

Reading the entreaty in her expression, he grimaced and set his fork on his half-empty plate. "It's awkward, isn't it?"

"What is?"

"Getting to know each other again. For some reason, I thought it would be easier."

She looked down at her lap. Hadn't this been why she'd resisted a meeting? Hadn't she known their special friendship would change with the end of anonymity?

"Erin." Brett leaned across the table and covered her hand with his own. "It wasn't a mistake. We had to do this."

She sighed. "So you keep saying."

"Trust me."

She looked at him gravely. "You're asking for something that's very hard for me to give."

Scowling, he sat back. "I've figured out that for myself."

She didn't know what to say to that, so she said nothing.

"So, tell me about your family," Brett prompted, obviously determined to keep the conversation moving. "I'd like to know more about your childhood. All I know is that your parents were divorced and your mother died several years ago. Have you always been very close to your brother?"

"Very," she replied, comfortable with that particular subject. "Adam is nine years older than I am. My mother had three miscarriages between us. My parents split up when I was only three. Adam was twelve and he became the 'man of the house' after our dad walked out. He was the one I turned to with my problems, the one who fixed my broken toys, the one who made sure I did my homework and brushed my teeth before bedtime."

"Your mother?"

"My mother had very little education and no job skills, having dropped out of school in her junior year to marry my father. She was always rather fragile physically, which, I think, was what attracted my father to her in the first place. But then she had those miscarriages and her health suffered. She had a very difficult pregnancy with me. The bills piled up and she became very depressed and she and my father started having problems. I don't remember those years very well, of course.

"Anyway, he left us with nothing but a few dollars in the bank, so Mother had to go to work. She found a job as a waitress in a cocktail lounge. It was very demanding work—too taxing for her, really—but she was afraid to give it up for fear of not finding anything else. She was very insecure about her lack of education and skills. She'd go to work late in the afternoon and come home very early in the morning. She slept during most of the days. Adam was the one who took care of me, on the whole, though I think Mother did the best she could. She was so tired all the time."

"What happened to her?" Brett asked gently, when Erin fell silent for a moment of painful remembrance.

"She insisted that Adam attend college when he graduated from high school, though he wanted to find a full-time job to support all of us so Mother could quit working. She convinced him that he could make more after obtaining a degree, so he attended a local college on a full academic scholarship. He worked after school and on weekends, but Mother refused to quit her job until he graduated."

"So your brother attended school, worked and took care of you. Quite a guy."

"Yes," Erin agreed proudly. "He is. It nearly broke his heart when our mother died two weeks after he graduated from college. I was thirteen."

"What happened to her?" Brett asked again, his eyes dark and sympathetic in the flickering light from the candle at the center of their table.

"Pneumonia," Erin answered simply. "She contracted it at work one night, but just kept going. By that time, she'd gotten into the habit of putting everyone but herself first and she waited too long to seek medical treatment. Adam was too immersed in finals and work to realize how sick she was—he's never gotten over that—and I was too young and too involved with my own adolescent problems. She collapsed at work one night. She never came home from the hospital."

"God, I'm sorry." His hand covered hers again, squeezing supportively. "That must have been a horrible time for you."

"I don't know what I would have done if it hadn't been for Adam."

"He raised you?"

"Yes. He got a job in a bank—a job he truly hated," she added with a grimace. "For the next five years, he dedicated his life to me, to making sure I didn't lack for anything, that I didn't get into trouble in school or elsewhere. He was a tough guardian, but I knew he loved me and I didn't rebel very often. When I graduated from high school, he gave me a bank book—the money he'd saved for my college education—and told me that he needed to go away for a while. He'd lived his life for my mother and me since he was twelve years old. He needed to do something for himself. He told me he'd always be there for me if I needed him, that all I ever had to do was call and he'd be here—and he has been."

"He gave you your independence."

Erin nodded, pleased that he understood. "Yes. Just as he claimed his own. I handled my freedom very well during my college years. I didn't get into trouble, kept my grades up, didn't get into the wrong crowds. After all, I had teachers and guidance counselors and dorm monitors to keep an eye on me, and that didn't bother me, because I was accustomed to answering to someone. And then, when I graduated with a fine-arts degree, I realized I was on my own. I panicked," she said frankly. "I'd gotten so used to having someone take care of me that I wasn't sure I could handle life on my own."

"Enter Martin," Brett murmured.

"Exactly. He was older and sophisticated and so very attentive that I was swept off my feet and into his arms almost before I knew it. He told me he wanted to take care of me. I wanted him to do that. It seemed the perfect match."

"You once told me you knew almost from the beginning that you'd made a mistake."

"I knew on my wedding night," Erin confirmed, looking away. "I found out then that Martin was basically selfish, that his own pleasure would always come first."

"You didn't sleep with him before you married him?"

Her cheeks burned and she looked quickly around to make sure no one had overheard. It had been much easier to talk frankly to Brett when they couldn't see each other. "No. I think he rather liked the idea of a young, virgin bride."

"The bastard," Brett muttered.

She smiled weakly. "Oh, yeah."

"But you tried to make it work?" It wasn't really a question; Brett knew Erin well enough by now to know that she would honor her commitments.

"Yes. I tried. And it wasn't too bad at first. As long as I provided Martin with the coveted trophy of a pretty young bride at his side for his many social functions, he treated me like a queen. But then I got pregnant. I was delighted. I thought the baby would finally give us a common goal, a common interest. He wanted me to get an abortion. When I refused, he told me that he was very sorry, but a baby simply didn't fit the plans he had for the remainder of his life. He left me when my figure started to go because of the pregnancy. He's never seen his daughter, though he's been very generous with his child-support payments. Never missed a one."

"He *is* a bastard," Brett said savagely. "How can you compare me—or any decent guy—to a shallow, selfish, lowlife creep like him?"

"I wasn't comparing you to him," Erin replied defensively. "Not really. I just know that most men aren't interested in women who have children."

"More bad experiences, Erin?"

"Yes. I've had men ask me out and then make excuses when I mention finding a baby-sitter. One man asked if I've ever considered boarding schools for my daughter. Boarding school! She's not even four yet."

"But, surely—"

"Oh, I know there are lots of nice, decent men out there," she said wearily, having heard that speech from Adam, Corey and Eileen so many times. "I just haven't been able to find them. I thought I'd met someone nice just over a year ago, but even he turned out to be more interested in his toys and things than in a little girl's feelings."

"What happened?" Brett asked, sounding resigned to hearing another story that cast his sex at a disadvantage.

"He asked me to dinner at his place one night after we'd been dating for several weeks. I think he'd planned to take me to bed that night. I—" She hesitated, blushing. "I was thinking along the same lines. After all, Scott was attractive and charming and he'd always been nice enough to Chelsea the few times he'd seen her. And it had been so long since . . . Well, you know."

"I know," Brett muttered grimly.

"Anyway, at the last minute, my baby-sitter canceled. I had to take Chelsea with me. Scott wasn't particularly gracious about it. During the evening, she got bored—as two-year-olds do—and she broke an expensive stereo component while investigating it. Scott lost his temper. I snatched her away from him just as he was drawing back to hit her. I replaced the equipment, of course—it took nearly a month's earnings to pay for it—and then I never saw him again."

"He would have hit a two-year-old child?" Brett repeated in disbelief.

"Yes. I'm sure he would have if I hadn't intervened. As I said, he was already sulking because the evening hadn't gone exactly as he'd planned. He accused me of bringing Chelsea along as a test—a way for me to find out what kind of father he would make before committing myself to making love with him."

"And had you?" Brett asked quietly.

Erin opened her mouth to furiously deny the question—and then stopped herself. "I don't know," she answered finally—something she'd never even admitted to herself. "Maybe I could have found another baby-sitter. Maybe I had reservations about going to bed with Scott without knowing where our relationship was leading. Maybe I sensed that there were things about him I wouldn't like, once I knew him better. I don't know. The point is, it has been better for Chelsea and for me since I stopped dating and concentrated on raising her."

"You haven't been on a date since that evening?"

She shook her head. "It just didn't seem worth the trouble."

Brett was silent for a long time. When he did speak, it was only to ask if she was ready to leave.

Glancing at her nearly empty plate, Erin wondered absently if she'd enjoyed the meal she hardly remembered eating. "Yes. I'm ready."

"Then, let's go." He threw some money on the table and held out his hand to her.

Studying his unsmiling expression, she placed her hand in his, wondering what he was thinking. Did he understand now why she was so reluctant to get involved with him? Was he going to tell her that he, like the others, wasn't interested in a woman who would always place her child first?

And had she really hoped, if only for a short time, that this one would be different from the others?

8

WHILE ERIN CHECKED on her sleeping daughter, Brett paid the teenage baby-sitter—generously, making the girl's eyes widen appreciatively. Erin waited until the teenager had left before turning to Brett in indignation. "You didn't have to pay for my daughter's baby-sitter. I would have taken care of it."

He only shrugged. "I asked you out. The evening was on me. Why does it bother you so much?"

Since she couldn't put her qualms into words—even to herself—she crossed her arms at her waist and turned away from him, her eyes on Chelsea's open bedroom door, concentrating on the dark silence inside the room. "It's getting late."

"We've talked on the phone much later than this."

She felt him moving closer, then knew that he'd stopped only inches behind her. "Do I make you nervous, Erin?" he asked with what sounded like only mild curiosity.

Her fingers tightened on her forearms. "No, of course not," she lied briskly, hoping he wouldn't notice that she was trembling like a leaf. *Nervous?* No. Somehow that mild, innocuous word didn't convey the half of it.

His hands landed gently on her shoulders and she nearly jumped. "Erin."

She closed her eyes, too vividly aware of how close he stood to her, of the warmth of his palms through her blue silk dress, the whisper of his breath at her nape. "What?"

"Would you look at me?"

She moistened her lips. "I—uh—"

His lips touched her neck. "Look at me, Erin."

Very slowly, she turned. He was smiling, his golden-brown eyes crinkled at the corners, his dimples carved deeply into his tanned cheeks. "Don't be nervous, Erin. It's only Brett."

Only Brett, who'd entered her life so unexpectedly and become important to her before she'd realized it. Only Brett, who'd made her want things she'd thought were long ago put behind her. Only Brett, who made her tremble with his smile.

He cupped her face in his hands, still gazing into her eyes. "I have a confession to make."

"You do?" She cleared her throat to make her voice less husky. "What?"

"I'm really glad you didn't wear high heels tonight. I'm not normally intimidated by women who are taller than I am, but—just for tonight—I'm glad you aren't towering above me."

She couldn't help smiling. "Why tonight?"

"Well, you see, I'm a bit nervous, myself. It makes it easier that we're on the same level."

"Why would *you* be nervous?" Erin asked, startled, half-skeptical about his words.

His smile deepened, and his eyes looked warm enough to melt her willpower. "You don't feel it?"

Standing very still, hardly breathing, she felt the fine tremors in the fingers cupping her cheeks. Brett was trembling, too! "Why?" she whispered.

He touched his lips to hers—a butterfly caress too brief to require a response. "I've never wanted anyone like this. I've never needed anyone this much. And I'm so afraid of doing something wrong, something stupid, something that would make you push me away."

His admission of uncertainty twisted her heart, further weakening her shaky resistance to him. She lifted her hands tentatively to his chest. She felt his heart beating beneath her palms, rapidly, forcefully. In response to her touch, he drew a deep, slightly ragged breath. His smile remained, but she saw the strain at the corners of his mouth. "Are you going to push me away, Erin?"

She should. She knew she should. But, oh, how she wanted to kiss him! To be swept again into that whirl of pure sensation she'd experienced earlier when he'd kissed her. Had memory exaggerated her incredible response to that earlier kiss? Would she react the same way if they were to kiss again? Would it be utterly foolish of her to try to find out?

She could only look at him, willing him to take the decision out of her hands.

His gaze still locked with hers, his mouth brushed hers again. A bit longer this time. A bit harder. Still, not nearly enough.

She almost moaned her frustration when he drew back. He wasn't going to make it easy for her, she realized abruptly. He wasn't going to make her decisions for her, leaving himself open to reproof later. She would have to make the first move.

Her fingers gripped the finely woven fabric of his shirt. Very slowly, she leaned toward him. He met her halfway, his lips curved upward in a satisfied smile when they touched hers. And then the smile was gone and he was kissing her with the same rapacious hunger she'd sensed in him earlier. And, as before, she lost herself in his need and her own. Her arms went around his neck even as his locked behind her. They strained together, mouths and tongues expressing everything they hadn't been able to say with mere words.

Madness claimed them both during the kiss. Unrestrained, uncontrollable madness. It swept away doubts, reservations, inhibitions, leaving in its wake only aching need. "So long," Brett muttered, clasping her fiercely against him. "I've wanted you for so long."

"Brett," she whispered. "I want you, too."

She couldn't remember ever wanting like this, ever needing like this, ever feeling like this. She wasn't certain she'd survive if she acted upon those needs, wasn't sure she'd want to if she didn't. She didn't even know if she had a choice.

Brett seemed to think she did. He pulled back only enough to allow him to see her face. His eyes were dark, turbulent. "Let me love you tonight, Erin. Please."

She caught her lower lip between her teeth, feeling torn. Feeling desire. Fear. Hunger. Uncertainty. Her gaze went to her daughter's bedroom door.

Following the look, Brett seemed to understand. "I won't be here when she wakes up. But please, don't send me away yet."

Through half-lowered lashes, she studied the face that had already become so familiar to her. She no longer felt as though they'd just met. He'd seduced her long before, in intimate, candid conversations, shared laughter, hazy dreams. Seduction of the mind, she realized, could be just as powerful as a conventional courtship. He'd made her want him before she'd ever seen him. Now she could touch him, taste him, feast on the physical attraction of curly hair and golden-brown eyes, masculine dimples and a flashing smile. And she wanted him even more.

She released a sigh of surrender. Or was it anticipation? "I don't want you to go. Not yet."

The words had been a mere whisper, but he heard them. His smile was blinding. He held his hands out to her, and she placed hers in them in an instinctive gesture of trust.

She led him into her bedroom, locking the door behind them, turning to him. The look in his eyes as he undressed her excited her. Her body seemed to delight him more with each inch he uncovered. His murmured praises rippled through her, taking away any shyness she might have felt. She stood proudly before him, letting him take his time exploring her with his eyes and his hands.

He paid slow, loving homage to her full, firm breasts, teasing them with his tongue, then drawing each nipple deeply into his mouth until she was forced to cling to his shoulders for support. Her head fell back and her eyes closed when his hair brushed her bare shoulders as he moved downward, his open mouth trailing a moist path from her breasts to her navel. He paused there only a moment, then dropped to his knees to nuzzle warmly at her thighs and the dark triangle between as he slowly lowered her hose and panties. She bit her lip to hold back a cry of pleasure and anguish, her hands clenching his shoulders convulsively. Unable to bear any more, she tugged at him, urging him back to his feet.

She was on fire when she reached for the buttons of his shirt, craving the feel of him against her. Eagerly she spread the fabric, exposing the warm, glistening skin beneath. His chest was sleek and tanned, and rippled with subtle musculature that testified to his healthy fitness. She drew her palms slowly down from his shoulders to his waist. He held his breath, his eyes heavy lidded, watching her as she'd watched him only moments before. She hoped her pleasure with his body was as obvious to him as had been his delight in hers.

The shirt fell unnoticed to the floor. Brett drew her closer until her breasts lightly brushed his chest. They both caught their breaths in ragged unison at the sensation. His fingers traced her spine from shoulder to hip. Then, molding his hands against her flesh, he pulled her even closer until their bodies were pressed together from breast to knee, with only the fabric of his trousers separating them. Even that was too much—she wanted all of him.

Reaching between them, she tugged impatiently at his belt buckle, making him laugh huskily and move back to give her better access. His laughter had died by the time his slacks and briefs dropped to the floor.

Just as he had explored her, Erin wanted to know every inch of the man whose mind she knew so well. She tasted the corded strength of his neck, feeling the pulse pounding there, reveling in his excitement. She lowered her head to sweep her tongue across his small brown nipples, feeling him flinch in response. He was sensitive there, she observed with delight, tugging delicately at one nub, then the other, with the edges of her teeth. His choked moan made her laugh breathlessly.

"Witch," he accused, bringing her hard against him as he sought and found her mouth with his. She thought fleetingly of the parts of him she had yet to investigate, but then the room tilted around her and she found herself on the bed, with Brett leaning over her. He murmured her name and she held out her arms to him, no longer doubting that this was what she wanted. He paused only long enough to ensure her protection from pregnancy, and then he covered her, his tongue surging into her eager mouth in a bold imitation of the more intimate joining to come.

It was as if it were the first time. New sensations, new emotions flooded her, carrying her higher than she'd ever been. And yet she was grateful for previous experience that had taught her ways of pleasing him in return. She was an active participant in their lovemaking, not a timid recipient. And she did please him. He left her in no doubt about that.

She'd never believed a man could be so generous, so unselfish in his lovemaking. So unconcerned over who was the leader, who the follower. He led her, yet seemed just as eager to grant her every unspoken wish. She'd never imagined her own greed could drive her so relentlessly, nor that her own hunger could make her so anxious to satisfy his.

Their limbs became fluid, their bodies sinuous, as they rolled, shifted, undulated—hands skimming, caressing; mouths seeking, sampling. There were husky moans and urgent whispers, pounding pulses and harsh, ragged breaths. It was pleasure that bordered the boundaries of pain.

Brett's fingers stroked the silky, moist flesh buried in the nest of curls between her legs and Erin arched with a pleading cry. She grasped the heavy, throbbing evidence of his arousal and he shuddered, growling her name.

"Now, Brett," she whispered, clutching frantically at his perspiration-dewed shoulders. "Please. Now."

"I know it's been a long time," he muttered, his muscles rigid with restraint. "I don't want to hurt you."

She wrapped her long legs around his hips and moved enticingly against him. "You won't," she promised. "I need you, Brett. Now."

He groaned and flexed forward. His mouth covered hers when she would have cried out in delirious pleasure, so lost in passion that she'd forgotten the need for discretion. Buried deeply inside her, he paused to allow her to adjust to him. Her heart beating against his, her body entwined with his, Erin opened her eyes to find him looking back at her, his glowing eyes penetrating the shadows surrounding them. And abruptly she realized that what she felt was more—much more—than desire.

Too afraid to put a name to the emotion swelling within her, she squeezed her eyes shut and concentrated on the physical, the definable. She tightened around him, lifting her hips in the initiation of a slow rhythm that he picked up immediately. His hands moved on her and rational thought fled, taking with it the fears that had temporarily assailed her. His head bent to her breast and she bowed beneath him, blindly striving toward something she couldn't understand, having never experienced it before.

"That's it, sweetheart," he murmured, his deep voice barely audible. "Let go. Just let go, Erin. Trust me."

Willingly surrendering the trust he requested, she clung to him in breathless anticipation. And then his fingers slid between them and her entire body strained in reaction. Her toes clenched, her breath locked in her throat, her face flushed with heat. She tried to cry out, but her voice was gone; she could do nothing more than gasp.

The powerful climax rocked her, rippling through her again and again. Hot tears blinded her to everything but the feel of Brett against her, inside her. She wanted to share those incredible feelings with him, wanted him with her on that higher plane of existence. She tightened her legs around his hips, pulling him deeper within her. His muffled groan signaled the beginning of his own release and then he was shuddering in her arms. Tears streaming down the sides of her face, Erin held him more tightly, her heart aching with the love she'd tried so desperately to deny, so vainly to resist.

Afterwards, they didn't sleep, but lay silently wrapped together, slowly recovering. With Brett's heart beating beneath her cheek, Erin closed her eyes and savored. How could she have known it would be like this? How could she have anticipated something she'd never even experienced in dreams? How could she regret knowing such ecstasy, even if only for this one time? She couldn't. Her only regret was that the end had come so quickly.

For just a little while, she hadn't been Erin Spencer. Hadn't been mother or sister or breadwinner or homemaker. For just a little while, she had been someone altogether different: a creature of passion, a woman conceived in fantasy, nurtured by love. She wouldn't—couldn't—exist in daylight, but, oh, these moments in the darkness had been glorious!

She smiled and nestled more deeply into his arms, knowing he would soon have to go.

Brett tightened his arms around her, wondering about her silence. Was she sorry that they'd made love? Did she have any regrets? Could she possibly understand the significance of what had happened between them?

Just remembering made his blood start pumping faster again, his body tense. Though he'd thought himself a man of experience—discriminating, but well practiced—he'd never known anything like what he'd just shared with Erin. He'd had sex before, even great sex on occasion. But he'd never made love until Erin.

Already he wanted her again, wanted to know if anything could possibly be that spectacular twice. But he had to go. And he still didn't know how she felt about what they'd done.

"Erin?"

She stirred lazily, stretching with feline grace. "Mmm?"

He reached out to snap on the small lamp on the nightstand, causing both of them to blink in its golden glow. "Are you—um—okay?"

She lifted her head to smile radiantly down at him. "Are you kidding?"

He began to relax. "Does that mean yes?"

Chuckling, she dropped a kiss on his lips. "That means I feel wonderful. Glorious. Fantastic!"

Brett blew out a deep breath and made a show of wiping his brow in relief.

Erin laughed softly. "You're so silly. How could you doubt how good it was for me? Couldn't you tell?"

"Honey, I'm still so dazed, I wouldn't be surprised if I'd dreamed the whole thing," he admitted.

She looked surprised, then pleased. "So it was good for you, too?"

Shaking his head in exasperated disbelief, he thought in disgust of her ex-husband. "Sweetheart, it was unbelievable," he assured her. "It's never been that good with anyone before."

What might have been skepticism crossed her face, but then she smiled. "You're very sweet," she told him before kissing him again.

He sighed. How was he supposed to convince her that he wasn't just telling her what he thought she wanted to hear? If he told her what he was really feeling, she'd probably bolt from the room in panic. He didn't think she was ready for the truth. "I guess I'd better go," he said reluctantly, glancing at the clock. "It's getting late."

"Yes." She sounded no more enthusiastic than he had. "How long will you be in town?"

"I haven't decided. I can probably take a couple of weeks off. It's really up to you."

Her eyes widened. "To me?"

He nodded without taking his gaze from her face. "Yes. Do you want me to stay that long? Will you arrange to spend time with me if I do?"

Chewing her lower lip in the gesture he'd already recognized as characteristic, she thought about the question. And then she seemed to reach some conclusion that satisfied her. "Yes," she told him with a nod. "I'd love to spend time with you during the next two weeks. Chelsea attends preschool in the mornings three days a week and I'm usually able to find a baby-sitter for occasional evenings."

He'd almost forgotten her daughter. Hoping she hadn't noticed, he caught her hand in his. "You don't have to find a baby-sitter every time. I don't mind if Chelsea joins us. I'd like to get to know her better."

Erin didn't answer.

Brett began to scowl. "Look, Erin, how many times do I have to tell you that I'm not like your ex-husband? I'm not worried about maintaining some sort of macho image that would be spoiled by the presence of a child. And I'm not like the last jerk you dated. I won't have a tantrum if Chelsea breaks one of my toys."

"I just don't think you understand what it's like to have a three-year-old around for long," Erin countered almost apologetically. "It's a very demanding age. Chelsea's exceptionally well behaved, if I do say so myself, but she's a normal child. She wants attention, and she's sometimes too curious for her own good and—"

"And I'd like to have a chance to find out about her for myself," Brett interrupted. "I'm sure she's as delightful as her mother."

Erin only smiled and kissed him yet again. This time he held her when she would have pulled away, making the kiss a deep, thorough one. He groaned when it ended. "If I don't leave now, I never will. Will you see me tomorrow?"

"Yes. I'll be here in the morning. Chelsea's in preschool from eight-thirty until noon."

He stepped into his slacks and reached for his shirt. "I'll drop by around nine, then."

"All right." She watched as he finished dressing, then walked him to the door. "Drive carefully."

He smiled at the advice that sounded as if it could have come from his sister. And then he kissed her until his ears buzzed, just to make sure she knew there was nothing fraternal about his feelings for her. "Good night, Erin."

"Good night." She watched him step outside, started to close the door, then opened it again. "Brett."

Running a hand through his disheveled hair, he turned on the walk, admiring the way she looked, silhouetted in the doorway in her thin, silky robe. "Yes?"

"I'm glad you're here," she said in a rush. "We're going to have such fun for the next two weeks."

And then she closed the door, leaving him staring wryly at its dark, unrevealing surface.

Fun. The word repeated itself in his mind as he drove toward his sister's house on the mostly deserted streets. It seemed that Erin had forgiven him for descending on her, was even welcoming his presence now. Why did he have the feeling that she was planning on taking a vacation, of sorts, and that he was the resort she'd chosen?

He wasn't particularly pleased by the analogy that had popped into his head. He'd go along with her for now, but he intended to make sure this was one vacation she'd never want to end.

AS PROMISED, BRETT arrived at Erin's house at nine the next morning. Precisely. Her heart beating faster, her stomach clenched in an unexplainable attack of nerves, she cleared her throat and smoothed her embroidered ivory sweater over her jeans before opening the door in response to his knock.

He looked wonderful—his thick hair wind-tossed into an unruly cap of curls, his trim, so-talented body clad in an oversize blue pullover and jeans so tight they were just short of shocking. "Good morning," she said, feeling strangely shy as her gaze met his smiling one.

"You're blushing," he observed in amusement, stepping inside to slip his arms around her waist.

His comment, of course, only made her blush deepen. "Have you had breakfast?" she asked, quickly changing the subject.

He laughed. "Hours ago." And then he kissed her. Thoroughly. "Good morning," he murmured when he finally released her mouth.

That quickly, embarrassment had become searing desire. She clung to his shoulders, trying to stiffen knees suddenly gone weak. "Has anyone ever mentioned," she asked huskily, "that you are one fantastic kisser?"

His eyes darkened. "Never so delightfully," he murmured, drawing her back to him for another long, devastating kiss. By the time it ended, they were both trembling.

Expecting to be hustled straight into the bedroom, Erin blinked in surprise when Brett cleared his throat, stepped out of her reach and waved vaguely toward the front door. "Are you ready?"

She was most definitely ready, but she wasn't certain they were thinking about the same thing. Following his gesture toward the door, she frowned and asked, "For what?"

"Are you ready to go? Need to turn off lights, or get your purse or anything?"

She hadn't known they were going anywhere. Looking longingly toward the bedroom, she stuttered, "Well, I—"

"I'll wait for you outside, okay? I could—uh—use some fresh air." And he all but bolted outside, leaving her looking after him in a mixture of frustration and bewilderment. Would she ever learn to predict this man? she wondered, even as she snapped on her answering machine and went in search of her purse.

Standing on the small porch outside her front door, Brett took several long, deep breaths of warm, late-September air, wishing he'd worn jeans that weren't quite so tight. His aroused state was rather painful, but he took comfort from the knowledge that it would ease. Eventually.

It had been a close call, he thought ruefully, running his fingers through his hair. He'd decided sometime during the night that Erin needed reassurance that he wanted more from her than sex; that they had more than that as a foundation for a relationship. And then he'd nearly blown his own plan by taking her right there on the floor of her living room. *Great willpower, Nash!* he thought in self-disgust.

He turned as Erin stepped out to join him, her beautiful face still a bit dazed and kiss-flushed. And the jeans that had just begun to loosen grew painfully tight again.

It was going to be a *long* day!

THEY SPENT THE MORNING at MacArthur Park browsing through the Arkansas Arts Center and the Museum of Science and History. Brett confessed, to Erin's obvious amusement, that he'd always been fascinated by General Douglas MacArthur, who'd actually been born in the building that now housed the museum.

"Why is it," he mused at one point, studying a studio portrait of the famed military hero, "that I always visualize him looking like Gregory Peck?"

"Possibly because of Hollywood casting?"

Grinning, he glanced at her. "Could be." And then he looked at his watch. "What time are you supposed to pick up Chelsea?"

Catching his wrist so that she could see the time, she sighed. "Soon. We'd better go."

"Yeah." Looping an arm around her waist, he walked with her through the exit. "We'll get the kid and then find a burger joint for lunch. One with a playground. I'll bet she likes those, doesn't she?"

He felt Erin stiffen against his arm, though he didn't release her. "I really wasn't planning on going out to lunch," she murmured.

"You have other plans for the afternoon?"

He studied her face as she prevaricated. "Well, not really, but—"

"Now you do." Without giving her time to answer, he urged her into the passenger side of his car and circled the hood toward his own door. He wasn't exactly sure why Erin seemed so compelled to keep him away from Chelsea, but he was becoming more determined to include her in their activities. How could he show Erin that he could accept her daughter when she never gave him a chance to even talk to the kid?

Reluctantly, as if sensing that his mind was made up and wouldn't be changed without a major scene, Erin gave him directions to Chelsea's preschool. Chelsea seemed surprised, but not displeased to find Brett accompanying her mother. "Hi, Brett! Look at the picture I drawed today."

"Drew," Erin corrected even as Brett examined the colorful drawing of stick figures.

"Chelsea, these are really good," he assured her. "And, trust me, I'm an authority."

Hanging over the seat back beside his shoulder, Chelsea beamed at his praise, but frowned at the wording. "What's a ath-auth—"

"Authority," he repeated clearly. "Someone who knows what he's talking about. I draw people like this all the time. I draw a comic book."

"Yeah?" Tilting her dark head in appraisal, she studied him with huge, dark eyes. "Like the ones Mommy buyed last week?"

"Exactly like the ones your mother bought last week," he assured her gravely, knowing Erin had probably purchased copies of *The Midnight Warrior*. She'd already admitted she didn't read any other comics.

Clearing her throat self-consciously, Erin slid into the front passenger seat and turned to her daughter. "Sit down and buckle your seat belt, Chelsea."

Grinning to himself, Brett waited until the child had complied before turning to look at her, his arm slung casually over the back of the seat. "Want to go out to lunch with us?"

Chelsea bounced twice in approval. "Yes, *sir!*" she answered eagerly.

"You choose. Where's your favorite place to eat?"

Erin groaned dramatically even as Chelsea unhesitatingly named a pizza parlor.

Brett looked questioningly at Erin. "Is there a problem?"

"It's not the best pizza in town," she answered with a grimace. "It's a place custom-designed for kids, and the kids couldn't care less about the food."

"It's really neat, Brett," Chelsea assured him anxiously. "They have games and rides and big puppets that sing and everything. You can play Skee-Ball and win prizes, too."

"Skee-Ball?" Brett repeated, rubbing his jaw. "Gosh, I really love that game."

Erin rolled her eyes. Chelsea clapped her hands. "What are we waiting for?" she demanded.

"We're waiting for your mom to say it's okay," Brett explained, his eyes focused on Erin's face.

She looked impassively back at him for a long moment. Then she sighed and nodded. "All right. Just don't say I didn't warn you."

He only smiled and started the engine.

9

IT WAS LATE AFTERNOON before Erin unlocked her front door, as Brett and Chelsea waited behind her. Chelsea's chubby hands were filled with plastic and stuffed toys from the pizza parlor's selection of prizes, and her face was streaked with the ice cream and candy Brett had insisted on providing despite Erin's protests.

"You might have mentioned," Erin said to Brett when Chelsea dashed to her room with her treasures, "that you'd been to that place a few times before."

Brett grinned. "How'd you guess?"

Erin shook her head, remembering his boyish enthusiasm in the game room, not to mention the money he'd spent on game tokens. Chelsea, of course, had been enthralled. "You tipped me off when you just happened to know the names of all the animated characters on the stage," she answered dryly. "As well as the lyrics to all their songs."

His grin deepening, Brett pulled playfully at a strand of her hair. "I told you Cheryl has two small boys, didn't I? I took my nephews there a few times last year when I visited them."

"I should have known," she said with a sigh. "I should have realized you'd love a place like that."

"I even like their pizza," he confessed cheerfully.

"I noticed." She had been amazed at how much he'd eaten.

"Speaking of food, you wouldn't have any cookies or anything, would you?" he asked, his expression reminding her very much of Chelsea's at times. "Skee-Ball makes me hungry."

She couldn't help smiling. "I'm beginning to think everything makes you hungry."

"You noticed that, too, huh?"

"Did you say cookies?" Chelsea asked from close behind them.

Brett grinned and caught Chelsea up in his arms. "My kind of kid," he informed her, making her giggle as he tossed her into the air.

Instinctively, Erin started to step toward them, but stopped herself just in time. It bothered her that Chelsea was so taken with Brett. She was hungry for masculine attention, having never known her father and seeing her only uncle so rarely. Erin was concerned that Chelsea would be hurt when Brett left. She couldn't even bear to think about how *she* would feel when he was gone.

Trying not to dwell on it, to just enjoy the moment for now, she turned to the kitchen to prepare snacks for Chelsea and Brett.

She hadn't intended for him to stay all day. But then somehow she found herself serving him a steak and salad for dinner while Chelsea chattered happily beside him. Brett was still there when Chelsea's bedtime arrived. Erin led Chelsea to her room, her thoughts already dashing ahead. Was Brett staying to make love to her? He'd been quite restrained during the day, but there'd been times when she'd caught him looking at her with an expression that had stopped her breath in her throat. She'd seen the sensual preoccupation in his eyes, and she had shared it.

And she was deluding herself if she believed she could resist him tonight, particularly now that she knew how fantastic they could be together.

Brett was waiting for her in the living room. He'd made coffee, she noticed. He smiled and nodded toward the cup waiting for her, patting the couch with his right hand to invite her to sit beside him. "You take cream and sugar, don't you?"

"Yes." She settled on the couch and picked up her cup, watching him from beneath her lashes. Lounging against the cushions, Brett looked completely relaxed. If he was only biding his time until pouncing on her, she reflected with a ripple of wry humor, it certainly didn't show in his expression.

"It's been a great day, hasn't it?" he asked, meeting her gaze with a smile.

"A very nice day," she agreed.

Holding his cup in his left hand, he reached out with his right to toy with a strand of her hair—a habit he seemed to have developed during the day. He twirled the dark curl around his finger, then released it, then twirled it again. "You have the softest hair. It's as fine and silky as Chelsea's," he murmured.

She didn't quite know what to say. She took a sip of her coffee.

"Tell me about your work," Brett said unexpectedly, abruptly releasing her hair to wrap both hands around his coffee cup. "How long have you been a commercial artist? Do you ever dabble in other forms of art? Do you have aspirations of being a world-renowned painter?"

Startled into a smile, Erin shook her head. "No. I'll never be a great artist and I'm content with that. I like what I do. It's quite a challenge to take my assignments and make them appealing to the average buyer. I like designing logos, too—coming up with something so eye-catching and unique that it will serve for years to identify the business or product. My friend Corey—I've mentioned her to you before, I think—"

Brett nodded.

"Well, she's a commercial artist, too, but she's the one with the real art talent. Her paintings are spectacular, but I'm afraid she still has a problem with self-confidence. Her family never encouraged her much and she had a professor in college who was a real . . . But you're not really interested in that, are you?" she asked, stopping herself when she noticed that Brett's gaze was focused on her mouth, his attention obviously elsewhere.

He frowned and quickly looked her in the eye. "Of course I am," he argued. "I'm interested in everything about you, including knowing about your friends."

"Well, we always end up talking about me," she argued, trying to ignore the ripples of awareness still cruising through her, all because he'd looked at her mouth. Simply looked at it, she reminded herself in mild disbelief. *Amazing.* "Tell me more about *The Midnight Warrior.* Do you still enjoy drawing it, even after two years?"

"I love it," Brett answered simply. "Those years I spent as a stockbroker nearly did me in. I never quite fit the image. Always drove the wrong car, wore the wrong watch, forgot what labels I was supposed to be wearing inside my clothes. Even worse—" he lowered his voice conspiratorially and leaned closer "—I don't like white wine. Or mineral water."

Erin raised a hand to her throat and looked seriously shocked. "How gauche," she pronounced in tones of dismay.

His eyes smiling at her teasing, he nodded gravely. "Yes, I know. Imagine the looks I got when I ordered domestic beer—or worse, Coke Classic—at the yuppie bars we frequented on Friday nights. And imagine the scorn I encountered when I admitted that my hobby was drawing cartoon characters."

Erin shook her head. "You must have been a real washout."

"Hopeless," he agreed solemnly. "I sold a lot of stocks, but of course that's only half the game in that sport."

"I read a couple of your comic books."

"Did you?" He smiled as if he hadn't already guessed. "Did you like them?"

She tried to think of a way to answer without offending him. "Well . . . they were very interesting. And the artwork was amazing. Do you do all the drawings yourself?"

"Yes. What didn't you like about the story lines?" He'd cut right through the "interesting" to the reservations beneath.

She shifted uncomfortably and avoided his eyes. "They're a bit . . . violent, aren't they?"

"In typical comic-book-adventure style, I suppose."

"And would a mild-mannered businessman suddenly turn into a midnight vigilante after the murder of his family? Don't you think this man is really in need of serious counseling?"

Brett only laughed at her hesitant questions. "It's fantasy, Erin," he reminded her. "Typical male-oriented fantasy of good taking on evil and winning one-on-one. Justice, retribution, triumph. I realize that good and evil are rarely as clearly defined as they are within the pages of the comics, but I think there's still a need for that type of escapist adventure. I'll bet you read romance novels," he added with startling accuracy.

Erin had to admit she did.

"And you accuse me of writing improbable fantasies?" he retorted, grinning cockily.

She lifted her chin. "At least women's fantasies don't usually involve mass bloodletting."

"You don't have to defend women's fantasies to me. I'm a great believer in fantasy in any morally and socially acceptable form. Sometimes I think our fantasies are all that keep us sane in an insane world. They're what keep us going, keep us striving, keep us optimistic even after reading a depressingly realistic newspaper from front to back. And, speaking of fantasies . . ." He scooted closer, his expression going from briefly serious to devilishly mischievous.

Holding her half-empty cup of coffee between them, Erin backed away. "Now, Brett—"

"Yes, Erin." Still smiling, he took her cup, set it on the low table in front of the couch and reached for her. "Now."

Obligatory protest out of the way, she settled into his arms with a sense of inevitability. Hadn't she known this was coming? Why not admit that she'd hoped it was? She lifted her face to his.

Fingers spearing into her hair, Brett exhaled deeply, his lips hovering only inches above hers. "I've been wanting to do this all day."

"I've been wanting you to," Erin confessed, sliding her hand to the back of his neck. "Kiss me, Brett."

His mouth covered hers almost before she'd finished saying his name.

Had it only been hours since he'd last kissed her? She threw herself into the embrace as if it had been days, weeks, even longer. He'd kissed her for the first time only the day before and yet she was already seriously addicted. How would she ever live without his kisses when he went back to Boston?

Shoving that depressing thought out of her mind, she snuggled closer into his arms, determined to enjoy every minute she had with him. She sighed into his mouth with pleasure when his hand covered one swelling breast. She fit him quite nicely, she observed, shifting to press herself more snugly into his palm. Thinking back to the night before, she realized contentedly that the words applied in many ways.

"Erin. God, how I want you." Brett's voice was ragged—the deep, husky voice of her telephone fantasy lover. Only then did it occur to her that he sounded quite different in person. She wondered why she hadn't noticed before. And then she forgot to wonder about anything as his weight shifted and they tumbled back into the cushions.

He was heavy and yet gloriously so. Delightfully crushed beneath him, Erin reveled in the sensation as he continued to move his lips over hers, his tongue probing the depths of her mouth. Her body, sexually reawakened after such a long deprivation, flared into overdrive, demanding the fulfillment she'd discovered only the night before. His arousal ground deliciously into her abdomen, telling her that he, too, sought satisfaction. She knew that in granting his, she would find her own.

She thought longingly of her bedroom, the privacy accorded by a locked door, the comfort and convenience of her big bed. "Brett," she whispered, turning her head to free her mouth. "Let's—"

"Mommy?"

The cry made Erin stiffen and her hands move immediately to push against Brett's shoulders. He groaned and rolled to the side, allowing her to slide out from under him.

"Mommy!"

Hesitating only a moment, she glanced at Brett, who lay on his back, one arm over his eyes. "You'd better see about her," he suggested, his voice still gritty from the arousal evident in his rigid body.

Her knees not quite steady, Erin turned and hurried to her daughter's bedroom, wishing she could have seen Brett's eyes. How was he reacting to this interruption? Had it made him more aware of the difficulties of dating a woman with a child? He'd been wonderful with Chelsea earlier, but Chelsea had been on her best behavior, so far. This was reality.

Chelsea was sitting up in her bed, whimpering, one hand pressed to her stomach, the other clutching Belle, the beloved doll Mrs. Price had made for her. "My tummy hurts," she whined the minute Erin stepped into the room. "Make it stop hurting, Mommy."

Erin sighed. She should have been more firm about the ice cream and candy, she thought regretfully, pulling the child into her arms. "Do you feel sick?" she asked, resting her hand against Chelsea's forehead, which felt damp, but cool.

"Maybe," Chelsea moaned, cuddling into her mother's shoulders to make the most of the attention. "It hurts," she repeated.

"What is it?" Brett stood in the doorway, silhouetted by the hall lights behind him.

Erin looked apologetically at him. It hadn't been anything she could have avoided. She'd been as eager as Brett to continue what they'd been doing. "She's not feeling well," she told him.

"What's wrong with her?"

"Her stomach's upset. Too many sweets and too much excitement, I think."

He grimaced. "Oh. Sorry."

"It's not your fault."

Chelsea moaned and buried her face in Erin's shoulder, her doll crushed between them. "I don't feel good," she whimpered, sounding queasy.

Erin looked again at Brett. "This may take a while."

He sighed and walked into the room. "Is there anything I can do to help?"

"Thanks, but no, there's really nothing you can do."

"Then I'll go and let you take care of her." He leaned over to brush a kiss lightly across her lips. "See you tomorrow?"

"I have some things to do tomorrow. Why don't you call in the morning and we'll see what we can work out."

"All right. Good night, Erin." He touched a gentle hand to Chelsea's back. "Good night, Chelsea. I'm sorry you don't feel well."

"G'night, Brett," Chelsea murmured without lifting her face out of Erin's shoulder.

Brett hesitated only a moment longer, then turned and left the room. Slowly rocking her daughter on the edge of the bed, Erin heard the front door close behind him, then the fainter sound of his car starting.

She should have expected this, she thought despondently, rubbing Chelsea's back with a tender hand. She'd known it would happen, of course, but had hoped she'd have at least tonight with him.

She'd fallen in love with him. Real love, this time—not the naive infatuation she'd felt for Martin. She'd probably loved Brett before she'd ever even seen him. She hardly expected anything permanent to come of this whirlwind affair. Nothing about their relationship had been predictable so far, from their initial contact to that unexpected meeting in the park. She didn't know what to expect from the future, except the certainty that their "affair" couldn't last.

She simply didn't know how to deal with a spontaneous, impulsive, footloose type like Brett, endearing as she found those qualities. She knew he wasn't shallow, materialistic and selfish as Martin had been; but would Brett be any more willing to sacrifice his long-accustomed freedom for a life of schedules, regular bedtimes, fun impulses dashed because of the lack of a baby-sitter?

Probably not.

Chelsea moaned and grabbed for her stomach. "Mommy?"

Putting Brett out of her mind to concentrate on more immediate concerns, Erin rose and, carrying her daughter, hurried toward the bathroom.

CHELSEA'S TUMMYACHE turned out to be stomach flu. It lasted forty-eight hours. Erin talked to Brett on the telephone a few times during those two days, but firmly refused to see him. She didn't want him exposed to Chelsea's illness, she said when he offered to come over, and she wouldn't leave her daughter when the child was ill.

"I'd understand, of course, if you have to get back to Boston now," she added, obviously trying to sound casual.

Brett informed her crisply that he would still be in town when Chelsea recovered. "This will give me a chance to visit with Cheryl and the boys," he added. "Why don't you and I plan to have dinner Friday night? Chelsea should be fully recovered by then."

"All right," Erin agreed. "I'll arrange for a baby-sitter."

"I'll call you tomorrow, okay?"

"Sure. Bye."

"Yeah." He hung up with a sigh.

"No one ever said parenthood is a glamorous job," Cheryl reminded him, having entered her kitchen in time to hear the end of the conversation. "I couldn't even tell you the last time Dwayne and I had a weekend to ourselves."

"I'm pond scum," Brett admitted, hanging his head.

Cheryl laughed. "Why is that?"

"I'm actually sitting here being jealous of a three-year-old kid with stomach flu."

Still smiling, Cheryl ruffled his hair, much the same way as she had when they were kids. "Don't feel too badly. Dwayne feels like that at times. There are just days when we moms have to put the kids first and the grown-up boys second."

Brett scowled at her. "You're patronizing me."

"Yes, I am. So, what are you going to do about it?" she challenged.

Nothing. Absolutely nothing. He was having a good time visiting his family and he'd be seeing Erin Friday.

He intended to make sure it was one evening she'd never forget.

ERIN CHECKED her appearance in the mirror. Brett had told her to wear something sexy. "Not that appearances matter, of course," he'd added, a smile in his voice. "I'd think you were sexy if you were wearing a garbage bag."

She wasn't wearing a garbage bag.

The dress was silver—a glistening, clinging fabric that hugged her from the deeply draped neckline to the knee-length hem. Diamonds glittered at her ears, throat and wrist, rhinestones sparkled in her upswept dark hair, silver sandals with impossibly high heels barely supported her silk-sheathed feet. Her gaze lingered on those sandals. They were definitely sexy. Much better suited to this particular dress than flats. But they would make her at least three inches taller than Brett. Would that bother him? Should she change?

The doorbell rang, letting her know she was out of time. She could still slip the sandals off and . . .

No. Shaking her head in irritation at her own waffling, she turned and headed for the door. She and Brett had agreed that their relationship was based on more than appearances, right? So the disparity in their heights shouldn't matter.

The bell rang again just as she reached for the doorknob. Brett was getting impatient, she thought with a secret smile.

She knew the feeling. It seemed like weeks, rather than days, since she'd seen him.

His eyes rounded when she opened the door. "Remember what I said about appearances not mattering?"

She smiled. "Yes."

"I lied. You're the most beautiful woman I've ever seen. And I love it."

She felt warmth flood her cheeks. She'd heard such compliments in the past, of course. But they'd never meant the same to her before she'd heard them in Brett's voice, before seeing the almost-stunned appreciation in his eyes. "Thank you. You look very handsome, yourself." He looked wonderful, she thought, studying the way his dark suit molded his athletically trim body as he walked past her into the room.

"Where's Chelsea?"

"She went over earlier for hot dogs and a Disney movie before bedtime." Erin had told Brett when they'd made arrangements for the evening that Chelsea would be spending the night with Mrs. Price, though Erin had promised to pick her up early Saturday morning.

"Good. Then I can do this." He slipped one arm around her waist and snagged the back of her neck with his other hand to bring her mouth to his. If it bothered him that he had to reach up a bit to do so, it certainly didn't show in his kiss. He stormed her mouth like a man who'd been starving for her, like a man who delighted in everything about her. She closed her eyes and responded to the embrace with very similar emotions.

Brett's breathing was discernibly accelerated when he drew back. Erin thought hers had stopped altogether.

Brett checked his watch. "Are you ready to go?" he asked huskily, and again she had the impression of impatience.

She nodded and reached for her purse.

They said little during the drive. Erin wasn't particularly surprised when Brett turned into the parking lot of a luxurious downtown Little Rock hotel. After all, the restaurant there was very good, and quite popular. She did lift a questioning eyebrow, however, when he led her to the glass elevators on the opposite side of the lobby from the restaurant entrance and pushed the call button. The only place she knew of upstairs was a piano bar on the top floor. Perhaps they were having drinks before dinner.

Instead, the elevator doors opened onto a floor of rooms. Grinning at her expression, Brett took her elbow and escorted her out of the elevator and down the hallway to a heavy wood door with a discreet brass number plate. He slipped a card into the lock.

Erin couldn't help smiling. Brett was obviously more impatient than she'd guessed earlier. He must have stopped on the way to her house to secure a room. She certainly wasn't complaining, but she'd thought they'd at least have dinner before they—

The sight that greeted her took her breath away again.

The suite's sitting room was gorgeous. Crystal and brass. A pale rose carpet so deep and soft she could have comfortably slept on it. An open doorway gave her a glimpse of a bedroom done in the same elegant theme. In the center of the sitting room was a small round table covered in white linen and beautifully set for two. Champagne cooled in a silver ice bucket. Flowers and candles were everywhere. From somewhere in the background, instrumental music played softly. Rachmaninoff.

She hadn't realized that her eyes had filled with tears until the room blurred in front of her and she was forced to blink to clear her vision. "Oh, Brett."

A trace of uncertainty, a touch of vulnerability that wrenched her heart, colored his voice when he asked, "Do you like it?"

She turned to give him a smile that trembled at the edges. "I love it. No one's ever done anything like this for me before." Though she didn't want to think of her ex-husband just then, she couldn't help thinking that Martin would never have arranged an evening like this. His pleasure in Erin had been showing her off to others, not sharing the intimacy of a candlelight dinner for two.

Brett caught her hand and lifted it to his lips. "I wanted to give you your fantasy," he murmured.

"You have," she whispered, as tears threatened again. "More than once." Didn't he know he *was* her fantasy?

Brett kissed her at the same time the discreet knock sounded at the door. He drew back, smiling. "Dinner is served, I believe."

They lingered a long time over the exquisite meal he'd ordered, talking quietly, savoring tastes and scents and the pleasure of being together.

The champagne bottle was empty, the dessert plates cleared away, the waiters gone before Brett rose from the table. The room seemed to flicker with the illumination of the dozens of candles arranged on every glossy surface, which were also reflected in the depths of his golden-brown eyes when he smiled down at her. And then he shrugged off his dark jacket, draped it over a chair and held out his hand. "Dance with me."

Smiling, she placed her hand in his. A seductively slow instrumental version of "Unchained Melody" had just begun to drift from the hidden speakers. Kicking off her shoes, she stepped into Brett's arms, closed her eyes and enjoyed, not particularly surprised to hear the tune, which was one of her all-time favorites. Such things happened in fantasies.

The carpet was too plush to allow for fancy steps. Erin didn't mind, and was content to sway in Brett's arms, her cheek against his, their bodies pressed so tightly together a breath of air couldn't have passed between them. His hand rested warmly at her waist, then slowly moved inward to the base of her spine, exerting just enough pressure to mold her hips more intimately to his. He was aroused, strongly aroused, but seemed in no hurry to end their leisurely dance.

His slightly ragged breath ruffled the fine hairs at her nape that had escaped her upsweep. She turned her head to taste the firm line of his jaw, her lips nibbling delicately at his smoothly-shaven skin. His responding groan rumbled deep in his chest, vibrating against her. His hand tightened on her back, then slowly slid downward to press against one firm, soft hip through the clinging silver dress.

Erin tickled his right earlobe with the tip of her tongue before catching it briefly between her teeth. Brett swallowed audibly, then released her hand, which he'd been holding in dance position, to place it against his chest before reaching up to her neatly styled hair. The rhinestone clips fell like glistening raindrops around their feet, unnoticed. Freed, her dark hair tumbled to her shoulders. He buried his fingers in it.

She worked her hand between them and tugged at the knot of his silk tie. She left it hanging loose and began to unbutton his shirt, still moving to the strains of the music, brushing her lips across his cheek. She felt Brett tugging at the long back zipper of her dress. She spread the sides of his shirt at the same time he lowered the dress to her waist and pulled her close again.

The low front of the silver dress hadn't allowed for a bra. She was glad, now, that it hadn't. Her unbound breasts, already swelling for his touch, brushed his bared chest, causing them both to shiver in sensual response. Erin slipped her arms around his neck, beneath the collar of his open shirt, bringing herself more snugly against him.

"God, I love being alone with you like this," he muttered, his arms drawing her even closer.

He was warm. So very warm. And strong. Pulsingly strong. She felt the ripple of muscles against her and luxuriated in the differences between male and female. How beautifully they meshed.

The song ended. Another began. In time to the new song—"Misty," Erin noted distantly—Brett rocked her against him. He pushed one leg between hers, making her aware for the first time that he'd lifted her straight skirt to allow him better access. Her silk-covered legs were exposed to midthigh. His hand slid beneath the hem of her skirt. He inhaled sharply when he discovered that she was wearing high-cut bikini panties, a frivolous scrap of a garter belt, and stockings—which left several inches of thigh bare to his touch.

"You meant to drive me to the edge tonight, didn't you?" he asked hoarsely.

"Yes," she answered, then caught his lower lip between her teeth.

Brett groaned and caught the back of her head to grind his mouth against hers in a kiss that sent the room spinning around her. The leg he'd inserted between hers thrust forward at the same time his fingers clenched into her buttock, rubbing her aching feminine mound against his rock-hard thigh. The blatantly sexual move made her shudder, and her fingers dug into his shoulders. "Brett!"

His eyes glinted wickedly when he lifted his head to give her a pirate's smile. "I hope you weren't planning on getting any sleep tonight."

"As a matter of fact, I wasn't," she assured him, her hips moving now without his guidance, her voice thick with a hunger for something totally different from the food they'd just eaten.

"Good," he replied, then covered her mouth with his again.

10

"I HAVE TO GET DRESSED," Erin murmured, expressing regret at bringing an end to the perfect night.

Brett's arm tightened around her bare shoulders. "Don't do that."

She smiled and lifted her head from his chest to look at him. "But I must," she informed him. "I have to pick Chelsea up at nine. I'd like to go home and change first. I don't think I want to go to Isabelle's door dressed in the clothes I left home in last night."

Shifting lazily against the pillows, Brett stroked his hand from her shoulder to her hip, dislodging the sheet that had covered her. "I'd like to keep you here—just like this—forever."

Still smiling, she brushed her mouth against his. "That sounds lovely. But not possible, I'm afraid. I've got a life to get back to. And so do you."

He sighed. "I guess you're right. Dammit."

Her smile faded. "Last night was the most beautiful night of my life, Brett. I want you to know that."

He slid a hand into her tousled hair and pulled her mouth down to his. "Thank you for telling me," he whispered against her slightly swollen lips. "It was for me, too."

The kiss was deep and tender. They'd kissed many times during the long, glorious night—too many times to count—and yet this one was different. This one said things Erin wasn't sure she was ready to hear. She drew back, shaken, her smile wavering. "I have to get dressed," she repeated, avoiding his eyes as she scooted toward the side of the bed.

The reflection she saw in the bevel-edged bathroom mirror made Erin moan in dismay. She looked . . . she looked . . . She looked as if she'd just spent a long night making strenuous, passionate love. Which, of course, she had.

She showered quickly, scrubbing away her faded makeup. Then she pulled a comb through her tangled hair and stepped back into the silver dress that was so appropriate for the evening, so unsuitable for the dawn. She carried a few cosmetics in her purse; she used them now to conceal, as best she could, the evidence of the long hours with little sleep. Studying her image again, she decided she looked better than she had earlier. Not her best, certainly, but at least presentable.

The blessedly welcome scent of coffee greeted her when she stepped back into the bedroom. Wearing a thick terry robe provided by the hotel, Brett smiled and held out a filled cup. "I thought you might like to have coffee while I shower," he said. "They just brought it up."

"Thank you," she breathed, eagerly accepting the delicate cup from him. "I really need this."

"I ordered croissants, too. Help yourself. I won't be long." Giving her a smile over his shoulder, he disappeared into the bathroom. Her gaze lingering on the closed door, Erin remembered a long, lazy bath sometime during the night in a marble tub that had simply begged to be shared. A shiver of arousal coursed down her spine. It would be a long time, if ever, before she could remember last night without reacting quite physically, she realized.

She heard the shower start as she stirred sugar and cream into her coffee. Sipping her coffee, she reminded herself that the night was over. It was time to get back to reality. And reality was Chelsea, probably waiting impatiently for her mother to come home.

Brett came back into the room with his hair damp, wearing only the slacks from his suit and his dark socks. In reaction, Erin's fingers clenched around her coffee cup, and suddenly she was all too aware of the wildly rumpled bed temptingly beside her. She tried to ignore it. "There's still hot coffee in the carafe," she said, hoping her voice sounded normal enough.

He slipped his arms into the sleeves of his shirt. "Thanks, but I had a quick cup while you dressed. I don't need any more right now."

She set her own empty cup on the table. "Then I guess we should go."

Shoving his feet into his shoes with somewhat more force than necessary, he nodded and reached for his coat and tie. "Yeah, I guess we should. It's almost seven."

She didn't like the sudden awkwardness between them, the uncharacteristic lack of expression in his eyes. It was as if he were deliberately distancing himself from her for some reason. Had he reached the same conclusion she had? That it was time to put the night behind them and get back to reality? That the fantasy had ended?

Casting one last look at the bed, Erin stepped into the sitting room and walked toward the door to the hallway. She'd just reached it when Brett's hand fell on her shoulder, turning her around to face him. Leaning into her, pressing her back against the door, he framed her face in his hands and kissed her until they were both gasping for air.

"Now we can go," he told her when he finally drew away.

She moistened slightly swollen lips with the tip of her tongue. "Yes," she repeated dazedly. "Now we can go."

As they walked out into the corridor and closed the door of the suite behind them, Erin wondered if anyone ever had the chance to visit paradise twice in one lifetime. Once a fantasy had ended, could it ever be replayed? Or was it destined to remain only in heartrending memories that would haunt her for the rest of her life?

BRETT WATCHED AS Erin unlocked her door. He'd already assured her that he wouldn't be staying, but he had no intention of leaving without one last kiss shared out of range of curious eyes. He noted with almost-idle interest that his body, thoroughly sated by a night of lovemaking like nothing he'd ever experienced before, still responded when she brushed against him as he held the door open for her. *Amazing.*

She turned to him as soon as they'd entered her living room. He couldn't stop looking at her. She was so lovely, even with her eyes a bit shadowy from a near-sleepless night, her hair falling in sexy disarray around her face and shoulders, her silver dress somewhat wrinkled. Those reminders of their night together only made her more beautiful to him.

He loved her. Last night had only confirmed what he'd already suspected. He loved her as he'd never even dreamed of loving a woman before.

He couldn't help wondering how that love was going to change his life.

Seeming to grow uncomfortable because of the intensity of his gaze, Erin glanced away. "I'd better change and get Chelsea."

"I know." He caught her hands in his, still unable to stop himself from staring at her lightly flushed face. "Dinner tonight?"

"I can't leave Chelsea with a baby-sitter again tonight."

He frowned impatiently. "Of course not. I'm not asking you to. We'll take her with us."

"I don't think so. After spending the night with Isabelle, Chelsea will need a quiet evening to settle into her normal routine. We'll probably turn in early. To be honest, I could use the rest."

He waited for her to invite him to join them for the quiet evening. His frown deepened when she didn't. "I'll call you later, then. Okay?"

She nodded and he thought he detected a hint of relief in her eyes. Had she expected him to push? "All right. Thanks again for the beautiful evening."

"No," he murmured, tugging at her hands to pull her close. "Thank you, Erin." He kissed her slowly, reluctant to step away from her.

She was the one who finally pulled back. "See you later, Brett."

"Yeah." He shoved his hands into his pockets. "See you, Erin." *The next time you'll allow it,* he added silently and with a degree of resentment that rather surprised him.

Maybe it was best that they spend a few hours apart, he decided as he backed his rented car out of her driveway. After their night of loving, his emotions were a little too close to the surface, a bit too raw. He could use the next few hours to regain some emotional distance, to think logically about what he wanted to do now that he'd acknowledged his love for Erin.

Cheryl was serving breakfast to her husband and sons when Brett let himself into her house. The family had obviously slept in on this nice Saturday morning. Brett was vividly conscious of his rumpled clothes from the night before as four pairs of curious eyes turned his way.

"So there you are," Cheryl murmured, grinning at Brett's expression. "Should I ask if you had a good time?"

Dwayne, the husky six-two redhead who'd married Brett's sister seven years earlier, shot a look of warning at his irrepressible wife. "Now, Cheryl, don't start on him."

Cheryl widened her brown eyes in exaggerated innocence. "But, Dwayne, I was only trying to make conversation."

"Yeah, sure you were."

"Did you go to a sleep-over party, Uncle Brett?" five-year-old Danny asked. "How come you didn't take extra clothes?"

"Didn't you even take your pj's?" four-year-old Kevin asked, studying his uncle's empty hands.

Brett cleared his throat, glaring at his giggling sister. "If everyone will excuse me, I believe I'll go change now."

"Why don't you do that," Cheryl agreed. "Then come back down and I'll make you something to eat."

Knowing he was in for an interrogation, Brett took his time changing into jeans and a cotton-knit sweater. He wasn't sure how much he wanted to tell Cheryl about his relationship with Erin. It would be nice to talk about it, share his confusion and uncertainty with someone who cared. But how could he put into words what he didn't understand completely himself?

He'd hoped her husband and children's presence would serve as a buffer—at least temporarily—from her questions. He was surprised to find her alone in the kitchen when he went back downstairs. "Where are Dwayne and the boys?"

"Dwayne had to run to the store for a part for the car. The boys went with him." She motioned him to a chair at the kitchen table and slid a coffee mug in front of him. "How do you want your eggs?"

"However you want to make them." He sipped his coffee, remembering that first cup he'd downed while Erin had showered and dressed. It had been all he could do then to prevent himself from joining her in the shower. He knew that if he had, they'd still be in the hotel suite.

He sighed.

"Want to talk about it?" Cheryl asked quietly, setting a well-filled plate in front of him.

He'd expected teasing, not obvious concern. He cocked an eyebrow in question. "Do I have a choice?"

"Of course, you do. Have I ever interfered in your life?" she asked indignantly.

He only looked at her.

She had the grace to blush. "Well, if you want me to stay out of it, just say so."

He reached across the table to pat her hand apologetically. "No, it's okay. I'm just a little shell-shocked this morning."

"Shell-shocked? Was the night that good?"

"Better," he muttered, spreading margarine on a slice of toast.

"This is getting serious, isn't it? I mean, really serious."

"It *is* serious. Really serious," he added in a weak imitation of her. "And I don't for the life of me know quite what to do about it."

"You're falling in love with her?"

"You may as well use the past tense. I fell. I tumbled. I went down for the count."

"You love her," Cheryl translated.

"I love her." He took a bite of toast.

"And?"

He swallowed the toast along with a slug of coffee. "And?"

"What *are* you going to do about it?"

"I—uh—I think I'm going to ask her to marry me," Brett answered slowly, as if even he didn't believe he was actually saying those words. He was rather dazed at hearing them coming from his own mouth.

Cheryl's lips twitched with the smile she considerately suppressed. "You think?"

"Well, yeah. I mean, it's only been a week since I first laid eyes on the woman," he temporized, dragging his fork through his eggs to keep from looking at his sister.

"So why did you really come to Arkansas, Brett?" she asked perceptively.

He sighed. "I think I came to ask her to marry me."

"Before you'd ever even set eyes on her?"

"Well, at least I came to see if the possibility existed that we— Oh, hell, Cheryl, I think I fell in love with her the first time I talked to her on the phone. It was like something just clicked—something I'd been waiting for for so long that I didn't have any trouble at all recognizing it when it hit me. I don't want to live without her anymore. I don't want our relationship to consist of telephone calls and stolen weekends. You know?"

She smiled tremulously, lovingly. "I know. And I'm so happy for you."

He grimaced. "Don't start throwing rice yet. I haven't asked her. I haven't even mentioned the possibility. I don't think Erin's even thinking beyond this weekend. She'd probably bolt in panic if I mentioned marriage."

"Because she doesn't know you well enough?"

"There's that. And she doesn't trust me," he added reluctantly.

Cheryl sat up straighter, immediately defensive. "Doesn't trust you about what?"

"Her daughter. She doesn't think I understand what's involved in raising a child."

Cheryl suddenly looked thoughtful. "Oh. I guess I'd sort of forgotten about Chelsea."

He grimaced. "I've done that once or twice myself."

"Oh, Brett. I can't say I don't understand Erin's fears. I'm a mother. I know what's involved. I know that you don't, because you've never had to deal with it. It isn't easy to raise a child. It's a full-time, lifelong commitment, taking precedence over everything else for years to come. You've been so footloose and responsibility free for the past few years. Are you sure you want to give that up for an instant family? Are you sure you can offer Chelsea the kind of love and commitment she deserves from a stepfather?"

Stepfather. The word made a bite of egg stick in his throat. Brett hastily washed it down, asking himself the same questions. He knew how he felt about Erin. He loved her. He wanted her. Always. And, to be painfully honest, he wanted her all to himself. He was selfish enough and newly enough in love that he wanted to smuggle her away from everyone else, wanted to hoard her like a treasure he'd discovered after years of searching. Sharing her with a three-year-old—a child who'd always take first priority with her—wouldn't have been his first choice.

But Chelsea existed, and Erin was a good mother. A wonderful mother. He admired her dedication to her daughter, the sacrifices she'd made to compensate for her poor choice of a father for her child. She wouldn't be the woman he loved if she were any different. Could Brett possibly be as selfless—for a child he hadn't fathered, hadn't spent nearly four years growing to love? She *was* a beautiful child—bright, inquisitive, well behaved, enjoyable. But he'd only been with her for a few hours. And already she'd come between him and Erin on more than one occasion. What would it be like to share Erin with her full-time? Would Chelsea be any happier about sharing than Brett was?

"I feel like a heel," he muttered, furious with himself for having such doubts. "No better than her selfish creep of an ex-husband."

"You're wrong there," Cheryl defended him firmly. "It's only human to ask yourself questions before taking a step this momentous, but you're nothing like the man you told me about. He's a shallow, insensitive, self-glorifying playboy. You're a kind, loving, generous man with a heart big enough to hold a dozen children if you choose."

"And you're just a bit biased," Brett reminded. He shoved his half-empty plate away and leaned both elbows on the table, looking to his older sister for advice for the first time in years. "What should I do, Cheryl?"

"The obvious answer is to spend more time getting to know both Erin *and* Chelsea," Cheryl answered briskly. "You'll never know how you feel about parenting until you give it a shot, will you?"

"Erin's not being particularly cooperative in that area," Brett admitted wryly. "She's worried that Chelsea will be hurt if things don't work out between us. She's had some unhappy experiences with guys treating Chelsea badly."

"Then the time you spend with them will also have to convince Erin that you know what you're getting into and that you can handle it. How long can you stay?"

"I can probably swing another week. But I hate to impose on you and Dwayne. I can get a room—"

"You'll do no such thing! We love having you here. You're my brother, for heaven's sake."

He smiled for the first time since sitting down. "Thanks, sis."

"You're welcome. And when are you going to introduce me to this woman?"

"Soon. I hope."

"Good. I'm dying of curiosity."

His smile deepened. "You'll like her, Cheryl. She's really very special."

Cheryl returned the smile affectionately. "She must be." And then she turned her head as the sound of car doors slamming came from outside. "Dwayne and the boys are home. So much for a chance to talk in peace."

Brett chuckled and stood to put his breakfast dishes in the dishwasher. Behind his show of amusement, however, lay a deep-seated concern about his future. Would he leave Arkansas a happy man, content with the family fate had brought him? Or would he leave a shard of broken heart behind if he and Erin couldn't work things out between them?

For one of the first times in his life, happy-go-lucky Brett Nash found himself afraid.

CHELSEA WAS ALREADY asleep and Erin had just gotten ready for bed when the telephone rang. Smiling at the familiar routine, she picked up the receiver of her bedside phone. "Hello?"

"I miss you."

Brett's deep voice coursed through her like the expensive champagne they'd shared the night before. She closed her eyes and gave herself up to the intoxication. "I miss you, too."

"How's Chelsea?"

It pleased her that he asked about her daughter so quickly, though she couldn't help wondering if that had been his intention. "She's fine. She and Isabelle had a wonderful time together last night. She's been talking about it all day."

"Is she asleep now?"

"Yes."

"And where are you?"

"I was just getting into bed," Erin admitted, curling her feet beneath her.

"So—uh—what are you wearing?" Brett inquired, hoarsely nonchalant.

She glanced down at her French silk nightgown with a slight smile. "Nothing much."

Brett moaned.

Erin's smile widened. "Is this an obscene telephone call?"

"It might become one if we don't change the subject. How about going to the fair with me tomorrow?"

"The fair?" Erin repeated, surprised.

"Yeah. The Arkansas State Fair. It's in full swing at the fairgrounds in Little Rock, you know. The boys have been talking about it all day. They wanted to go tonight, but Cheryl and Dwayne had to attend some kind of awards ceremony for the police department. I kept the little monsters for a couple of hours. Anyway, Dwayne has to work tomorrow, but as a bribe for one entire evening of exemplary behavior, I promised the boys I'd take them to the fair tomorrow afternoon. I'd like for you and Chelsea to come, too."

"I—uh—"

"It'll be fun. I love fairs. And Chelsea will like the boys. They're pretty decent kids. In fact, she can bring a friend and they can have a munchkin double date. What do you say?"

"I can't believe you're trying to fix up my three-year-old daughter," Erin accused him, swallowing a laugh.

"Hey, she and Kevin will be perfect for each other. Trust me. Of course, he's a little young to get a job—he's only four—so they'll probably have to move in with you after they're married, but I'm sure you're about ready for grandkids to spoil, right?"

The laugh escaped in a ripple of giggles. "You're insane, do you know that?"

"It's been suggested a few times. I like to think of it as artistically eccentric. So, is the answer yes?"

"Yes," she replied, quickly, because she really wanted to go. Chelsea would love the fair. And Erin would be with Brett again. How could she turn him down?

"Guess we'd better get some rest," Brett suggested, obviously reluctant to end the call. "Three kids under six at the fair may be just a bit strenuous."

"Oh, just a bit."

"Good night, then. Dream of me."

"I have been. For months," Erin murmured. Something about Brett made it hard for her to remember to be circumspect.

"Damn, I wish I were with you." The words were little more than a groan.

There was a long moment of silence, and then Brett muttered a hasty "Good night" and hung up.

Erin was breathing raggedly when she recradled her own receiver. She turned with a sharp exhalation to bury her face in a pillow, trying to pretend she was snuggling into Brett's arms.

ALMOST BESIDE HERSELF with excitement, Chelsea could hardly stand still long enough for Erin to help her dress for the fair. These last September days were warm, though the nights were turning cooler. To accommodate the weather, Erin dressed her daughter in layers of brightly colored knits, folding a jacket into the tote bag she would carry at the fairgrounds. She looped Chelsea's silky dark hair into a neat French braid to keep it out of the way, clipping a hot-pink bow at the nape. "You look adorable," she said, indulging herself with one long hug.

Chelsea wriggled impatiently. "Is it time to go yet? When's Brett going to be here?"

"Soon," Erin promised, standing to smooth her light-weight purple-splashed black sweater over her black acid-washed jeans. She put a hand to her own French braid to make sure it was still neat. It was.

"Can I take Belle? She'll love the fair."

"I'm afraid she would get dirty, Chelsea. Why don't you just tell her all about it when you get back?"

Chelsea sighed but agreed. "Maybe Brett will win me a teddy bear," she said. The ragged three-foot-tall stuffed dog Adam had won for her on a brief visit last year sat proudly in a corner of her bedroom.

"Now, Chelsea—"

The doorbell rang before Erin could deliver the lecture she'd intended. "Just don't pester Brett to play the games, you hear?"

"Yes, ma'am. Aren't you going to get the door?" Chelsea hopped from one sneakered foot to the other as she pushed her mother.

Erin headed for the door. She could only hope Brett's nephews proved enough distraction that Chelsea wouldn't drive Brett crazy with demands for his attention.

Danny and Kevin, two cute denim-clad redheads who hadn't yet entered the girls-are-yucky stage, took one look at dark-haired, dark-eyed Chelsea and fell in love. Both of them. A spirited competition for her attention began almost immediately. Erin smiled, aware that Chelsea would be quite happily diverted for the afternoon.

Brett grinned cockily, watching his nephews' macho posturings. "What'd I tell you? You should have brought another hot babe. Chelsea's going to have her hands full."

Erin watched as Chelsea smiled through long, dark lashes at Kevin before turning with interest to Danny. "I think she can handle it," she remarked dryly.

"I can tell we're going to have to keep a close eye on her in the future," Brett murmured, then immediately opened the door. "Ready to go? We're burnin' daylight," he added in his best John Wayne imitation.

Dazed by his subtle insinuation that he'd be around in Chelsea's future, Erin smiled weakly and reached for her tote bag before herding the children outside to the car. She decided not to think about his words at the moment. She'd save them for later, when she was alone.

ERIN HAD ALWAYS LOVED the fair. The smells and sounds took her back twenty years to her own childhood, when Adam had escorted her and her mother around the midway, making sure Erin had every snack she craved, rode every ride, owned every prize he could win for her. Staring at the crowded merry-go-round, she could almost see herself sitting on a pink horse beside her rather embarrassed teenage brother on his purple one. She blinked back tears.

"Erin? What's wrong?" Brett demanded.

She smiled and shook her head. "I was just thinking of times I used to come to the fair with Adam. He was so sweet to me. I thought he was the best big brother in the world. I think he must have been."

Brett took her hand, keeping his eyes on the three hand-linked children hurrying through the sawdust just ahead of them. "You're really close to him, aren't you?"

"He was the closest I had to a father when I was growing up," she answered candidly. "I adored him. I suppose it's safe to say I still do. He made so many sacrifices for me. Took care of me so well."

"He let you marry Martin," Brett grumbled.

"He couldn't have stopped me," she assured him.

Brett grimaced in mute apology. "Sometimes I'm a bit jealous of him," he admitted.

"Jealous of my brother?" Erin repeated in astonishment. "Why?"

"I guess you'd have to hear the way you talk about him to understand. So, where do you think the kids would like to begin? Rides or animal exhibits?"

"Rides!" all three children simultaneously cried out.

Brett grinned and allowed himself to be guided through the crowds toward the section of small-children's rides. While he was busy convincing Danny that some of the larger rides were too dangerous for five-year-olds, Erin considered what he'd said about Adam.

Seconds later, she decided she'd think about that later, too. She had the entire afternoon to spend with Brett. She wasn't going to spoil it by analyzing everything he said.

11

THEY STAYED AT THE FAIR until after dark. Even then, they had to practically drag the grubby, exhausted children away. Brett carried Chelsea to the car, both boys stubbornly proclaiming they were too old to be carried. All three were asleep before Brett had navigated the crowded, narrow Roosevelt Road to the freeway that would take them into North Little Rock.

"They're out," Erin stage-whispered, looking over her seat at the snoozing trio in the back, held upright only by their seat belts as they nodded bonelessly, surrounded by stuffed animals, balloons and toys. Brett had spent a small fortune on the kids, refusing to allow Erin to contribute a dime. She knew none of the children would ever forget this outing.

"Whew!" Brett breathed. "I didn't think they'd ever run out of energy. Lord knows, I did a long time ago."

She smiled. "I thought you kept up admirably well."

"I was trying to impress you with my stamina," he replied with a suggestive grin.

"You did that Friday night," she shot back, making him laugh softly and reach for her left hand with his right.

"You're good for my ego, Erin Spencer," he told her, bringing her knuckles to his mouth to brush them with his lips.

Her fingers curled around his.

None of the children awoke when Brett pulled into Erin's driveway and killed the engine. He walked around the car to open the back door. Handing Erin Chelsea's goodies in the big plastic bag they'd obtained at the Hall of Industry, he unbuckled Chelsea's seat belt and slid his arms beneath her. He lifted her without waking her, nestling her head into his shoulder. Erin had to swallow a sudden lump in her throat at the sight of him holding her daughter so comfortably.

"The boys will be okay while you carry her in?" she asked, looking at his sleeping nephews. "I really can manage her alone if you—"

"They'll be fine," he assured her. "I'm only going to carry her inside and then I'll come right back out. Besides, your hands are full."

She had to admit he was right. Between the tote she'd carried and the stuff Chelsea had hauled home, she never could have made it alone, despite her claim.

Following Erin's instructions, Brett deposited Chelsea on her bed on top of the bedspread. "I'll have to clean her up and change her into pajamas," Erin explained, setting the enormous bear he'd won next to the big dog in the corner of the room. There was something symbolic about Brett's prize sitting next to Adam's in her daughter's room, she was sure, but she was simply too tired to think about it now.

"Guess I'd better go, then. Cheryl will be worrying about the boys."

Erin walked him to the front door. They lingered there in a moment of silence, the usual disinclination to part hanging between them. It was getting harder each time to say good-night, and Erin read the same sentiment in Brett's sober eyes. "Thank you for taking us today," she told him, clinging to his hand. "Chelsea had a wonderful time, and I did, too."

"Me, too," he agreed. "Even when I nearly got sick on the Tilt-A-Whirl ride with Danny."

She smiled faintly, remembering how green Brett had looked when he'd staggered off the ride. Only then had he admitted that he had problems with rides that spun in circles. She'd thought it sweet that he'd ridden a "grown-up" ride to please his oldest nephew even though he'd known it would be difficult for him. "You were wonderful," she assured him.

"I wasn't half-bad, was I?" he replied cockily. "Did you hear that woman tell me what a good father I was?"

"Yes, I heard her." Erin clearly remembered the incident. Kevin had tripped over a power cord and scraped his hands. Obviously embarrassed to cry in front of Chelsea, whom he was trying so hard to impress, he'd turned to Brett for help. Brett had scooped the boy onto his shoulder and headed for the rest room, "To help him wash up," he'd called back, giving Kevin a few moments of privacy to recover.

Having seen the whole thing from her booth, one of the fair employees had complimented Brett when he'd returned with a smiling child. "I've seen fathers yell at their sons for crying and making the kids even more humiliated," she'd added, scowling. "Nice to see a young dad like you who understands that sometimes a kid needs to cry without being embarrassed about it."

Brett had blushed faintly with pleasure, twisting Erin's heart with pride for him. It hadn't been the only time during the evening they'd been taken for a family. There'd even been a few raised brows that Erin had interpreted as consternation at how closely the three children were spaced. She might well have had another child soon after Chelsea, as Brett's sister had done having her two, if Martin had been the type of man who loved children the way

Erin did. Many times she'd regretted that Chelsea might never have a brother or sister. Erin had thought her longing for another child had been put firmly behind her. Admittedly her maternal instincts were as active as ever.

These were very dangerous thoughts, she decided, shoving them away. "You'd better go. The boys will be frightened if they wake up alone in the car," she urged him.

"I know. I'm leaving." He kissed her, then opened the door. He'd just stepped outside when he turned and looked back at her. "Erin?"

"Yes?"

"What do *you* think about what that woman said? Do you think I'd be a good father?"

"I—uh—" Her throat tightened. Just how was she supposed to answer? Was his question only hypothetical or did he have something more personal in mind? "I think you'd make a wonderful father," she answered honestly. "If you'd decided that was what you wanted."

He smiled, obviously pleased. "Thanks. I'll call you tomorrow."

"All right. Good night, Brett." She closed the door before he could make any other unsettling remarks.

She thought about his words as she undressed her sleepy daughter and used a soapy washcloth before placing limp, weary limbs into the sleeves of a pair of soft pajamas. "Good night, sweetheart," she murmured, putting her partially clean child into bed and kissing her chubby cheek.

"Night, Mommy," Chelsea mumbled, half asleep. "I liked the fair."

"I'm glad. See you in the morning."

"Mommy?" Chelsea asked just as Erin was about to step out of the room.

"What is it, Chelsea?"

"Could Brett stay with us forever? I like him."

It must be the night for questions that knocked the breath right out of her, Erin thought, her hand tightening on the doorknob. "We'll—um—we'll talk about it later. Okay, sweetie? Go to sleep now."

"Okay. I love you, Mommy."

"I love you, too, baby."

Just what was Brett planning for them? Erin asked herself as she lay in bed later, staring at the darkened ceiling, so tired and yet too disturbed to sleep. She knew Brett would have to go back to Boston soon, though he'd avoided the issue so far. What then? A long-distance affair? Would either of them be content with their frequent telephone calls, perhaps an occasional visit? Would he ask her to go with him when he left? He hadn't mentioned marriage, hadn't even told her he loved her. So, what had he meant by that question about whether he'd make a good father?

Did Brett love her? There were times when she was convinced he must. The way he looked at her, the way he touched her, the way he'd made love to her Friday night— all night. Yet he'd never said the words.

She loved him. More deeply each hour she spent with him. She couldn't bear the thought of parting from him, going back to knowing him only as a voice over the telephone line. And yet—marriage? Uprooting herself and her child from the only state either of them had ever lived in and moving to a new town to start a new life with a man she had known such a relatively short time? How could she even think about doing that? Chelsea would be devastated if things didn't work out after such a drastic step. And Erin would very likely be destroyed by the shattering of another dream.

She tried to calm herself with the reminder that Brett hadn't asked her to marry him, that she was anticipating problems. Somehow she didn't find much comfort in that. If not marriage, what did he want for them? Or did he intend to tell her goodbye for good when he left Arkansas? Had this only been a vacation affair, a pleasant interlude before getting back to his real life? No, she couldn't find any comfort at all in that possibility.

The telephone rang at ten-thirty, just as her eyes were drifting shut. She turned to reach for the phone. She hadn't expected Brett to call tonight. She wasn't sure if she was pleased that he had. "Missing me already?" she asked lightly, trying to hide her anxiety behind flippancy.

"I miss you frequently," the male voice answered dryly. "But for some reason I don't think that question was directed at me."

She relaxed into the pillows. "Adam! I wasn't expecting it to be you."

"Obviously. So who did you think it was—as if I didn't know?"

"Brett," she admitted. She'd told Adam Brett's name several weeks earlier, after learning it herself, though she'd warned her brother then that she still didn't want him interfering in the unusual relationship.

"Yeah. That's what I thought. So your telephone romance is still going strong, I take it?" He made little effort to hide his disapproval.

"It's a little more than that now," Erin conceded. "Brett's here. Well, not *here*, but in Arkansas. He's staying with his sister."

There was a moment of silence, and then, "How long has he been there?"

"A week yesterday."

"How long's he staying?"

"I'm . . . not sure. Another week, maybe."

"And?"

"And what?"

"What's going on between the two of you?"

Erin bristled. "That's really none of your business," she told him crisply.

"Look, it's only natural that I would have concerns about this. It's not like this is the most normal courtship on record, you know. I mean, he seems okay—makes a good living, stays out of trouble, pays his bills and taxes—but you really don't—"

"Dammit, Adam, you checked him out, didn't you?" Erin interrupted furiously. "You promised you wouldn't do that."

"No," he reminded her. "I didn't. You ordered me not to, but I never promised I wouldn't."

"Why?"

"Look, Erin, I've been watching out for you since you were a baby. Just because we don't see each other very often now doesn't mean I can break that habit. I let you down with Martin. I don't want to see you get hurt again."

"You didn't let me down, Adam," Erin argued, remembering that Brett, too, had implied that Adam should have interfered with her disastrous marriage. Why couldn't either of them see that she had to make her own mistakes, had to be responsible for her own life? That she was an adult, capable of taking care of both herself and her child?

"Erin, I love you. I'm concerned about you. Is that so terrible?"

Weakened, as always, by his sincerity, Erin sighed. "No, Adam. It's not terrible. I love you, too, even when you're being arrogant and overprotective. But you have to let me make my own decisions, Adam. Give me credit for knowing what's best for me, will you?" She could almost laugh at her own words—she only wished she *did* know what was best for her.

"All right. So tell me about Brett. What's he like?"

She smiled. "He's wonderful. Funny and charming and thoughtful."

"Does Chelsea like him?"

"Very much. Particularly after today. He took us to the state fair. His nephews came along. They're five and four and they both want to marry Chelsea."

Adam groaned. "You mean, now I have to start worrying about her love life, too?"

She laughed. "It's okay, Uncle Adam. I think you've got a few years before you have to worry seriously about her."

"So the fair was back in town, huh? I'm sorry I couldn't have been there to go with you this year."

"So am I. I thought of you often today."

"I'm glad." There was a comfortable pause filled with happy memories before Adam spoke again. "You'll call me if you need me for anything?"

"Of course I will. Are you going to be in the country for a while?"

"A few more weeks, probably."

"Good. I hate it when you leave. I always worry so about you."

"I know. It comes with the territory of family."

"Yes," she agreed, catching his hint. "I know it does. I love you, Adam."

"Love you, too, sis. Just be careful, okay?"

"You, too. Bye."

"Yeah." He hung up without further comment—Adam never said goodbye.

Surprisingly enough, Erin fell asleep quickly after Adam's call. The questions, the worries were there at the back of her mind. But she pushed them aside, choosing, instead, to snuggle into the warm feelings remaining from a day with Brett and a call from her brother.

THOSE QUESTIONS and worries haunted her during the next few days, when Brett seemed determined to insinuate himself into her life as deeply as possible. Painfully aware of how much she'd miss him when he was gone, Erin tried at first not to get too accustomed to having him around. She quickly gave up that effort as futile. She loved having him around. She wanted him around all the time.

Twice during the week he took her out alone, leaving Chelsea with a baby-sitter. The other nights he spent at her house with the two of them, sharing meals and television programs, staying after Chelsea's bedtime to make love with Erin until—in deference to Erin's wishes—he forced himself to leave before Chelsea awoke.

FRIDAY MORNING, while Chelsea was in preschool, Erin drove into west Little Rock for her appointment with her optometrist, guiltily aware as she did so that she'd been letting her work slide while Brett was in town. She had to get busy again to make her deadlines and earn the salary she needed to support her daughter. She suspected that Brett would be leaving Sunday or Monday. She'd get right back to work after he left. She would need the work to keep her from sitting around missing him.

"Well, you were right, Erin. Your prescription does need to be changed," the optometrist, an attractive blonde in her early thirties, confirmed an hour later. "No wonder you were having headaches after a day at the drawing board. Your eyes were going into accommodation spasms."

Erin smiled at the woman who'd been taking care of her eyes for several years. "I won't even ask what that means."

"I'd be happy to explain," Dr. Spring McEntire assured her, sitting back on her stool with a smile, and indicating a technical-looking chart on her clipboard.

Erin shook her head. "I probably wouldn't understand if you did. Just write me a prescription and I'll wear the glasses."

The other woman laughed. "It's nice to know you have such faith in my judgment."

"Why shouldn't I?" Erin countered. "You've never given me any reason to doubt you." She looked around the examining room, smiling at the photograph displayed proudly on a shelf above the desk. "Your son is really growing," she remarked, studying the golden-haired, four-year-old sitting in a handsome blond man's lap, both of them dressed in bright, eye-catching colors. "He looks exactly like his father, doesn't he?"

"Identical," Spring agreed with a wry smile. "And they're just alike in other ways, too. I've really got my hands full with the two of them."

Erin had met Spring's husband socially a time or two and knew that the well-respected psychologist was a bit eccentric, to say the least. She also knew that the couple had been happily married for several years.

She remembered sharing a table with them at a country-club New Year's Eve party the year she and Martin had been married. Erin had envied their closeness and love for each other—something that had been missing almost from the beginning in her own marriage. Spring had been pregnant then. Erin had particularly craved the kind of joy the other couple had shared during that pregnancy. It was something that would be denied her throughout her own, which had begun by accident only two months later. Several times during those lonely, unhappy months, she'd thought of Spring and Clay McEntire, longing for the sort of love and support they'd shown each other.

"How's Chelsea?" Spring asked as she scribbled something on a prescription pad. She'd given Erin's daughter her first eye examination only a few months earlier.

"She's fine, thank you."

"She's a beautiful little girl," Spring complimented. "I'm hoping for a girl this time, though of course it doesn't really matter what we have, as long as it's healthy."

Startled, Erin looked at the other woman's flat waistline. "You're pregnant?"

Spring smiled brightly. "Yes. Three months."

Vague feelings of envy became outright jealousy. "That's wonderful news. I'm very happy for you." Erin forced a smile.

"Thanks. Clay's been wanting a second child ever since Easter when my family had a reunion and my sisters both brought their new babies, both girls. He played with my nieces all afternoon and has been dropping hints ever since. Even Sean's been nagging me for a baby brother or sister, though I think he's leaning toward a brother. Between the two of them, it wasn't too hard to talk me into it."

Erin took the prescription Spring held out to her and reached for her purse, still wearing her determined smile. "I really am happy for you," she repeated. "Give Clay my best, will you?"

"I will. Let me know if you have any trouble with those glasses, okay?"

"Yes, I will. Thanks, Spring."

Erin handed a check to the dark-haired woman at the front desk and left the office, still smiling. The smile faded the moment she slid behind the steering wheel of her car and closed the door. She couldn't help thinking again of

how very much she would like for Chelsea to have a baby
brother or sister. She couldn't help worrying again that it
would never happen. Brett was the only man she could
even imagine having children with—and yet, conversely,
she was terrified to make that commitment to him.

She groaned and started the car.

"CAN WE REALLY GO in an airplane, Brett?" Chelsea asked
excitedly from the back seat of the car.

He smiled at her in the rearview mirror. "We won't be
going up in the air in one," he reminded her. "But I understand there will be air-force planes on display that we
can go through. It'll be fun."

"And then we can see the Thunderbirds?"

"Yes. Then we can see the Thunderbirds," he promised.

Smiling, she hugged her doll and looked out the car
window, counting the minutes until they reached the Little Rock Air Force Base, which was holding its annual open
house and air show. Having read about the event in the
local newspapers, Brett had assured Erin and Chelsea that
they'd love it, particularly if he was the one escorting
them. Chelsea had been only slightly disappointed that his
nephews weren't accompanying them this time. Brett had
explained that the boys were planning to go the next day
with their parents, and had added that he hoped Chelsea
wouldn't mind too much.

Chelsea had smiled, given Brett a hug and assured him
that she would have a wonderful time with him and her
mom. He had only to remember that hug to experience
again the warm feelings it had sent through him. He could
easily get used to this little girl's hugs. Just as he had her
mother's.

He glanced over at Erin. She'd been awfully quiet today. What was bothering her? Was she aware, as he was,

that their time together would have to end soon—that he had to get back to Boston within the next few days? He wanted to think she dreaded that separation as much as he did. He wanted to believe there was a chance she would go with him when he left, though he hadn't yet had the nerve to make that suggestion. He intended to find that courage today. He was going to charm the socks off her today, show her again what a terrific father he'd make for her daughter. And tonight he planned to ask Erin to marry him.

Just thinking about her answer made his hands tremble on the steering wheel. Would it be yes? Or was she going to break his heart with a no?

"Looks like it's going to be crowded," Brett commented, subtly urging Erin to talk to him as he drove past the front gates of the base.

"Yes. Very crowded."

Clearly something was bothering her and he couldn't ask now, with Chelsea listening so avidly to everything they said.

Chelsea didn't seem to mind standing in long lines waiting to walk through the transport planes on display for the public. Clinging to Brett's hand, oblivious to the heat of the afternoon sun, she chattered nonstop about everything she saw. She could hardly wait for the air show. Brett had explained about the air-force flying team, the Thunderbirds—six F-16 jets flown by the best pilots in exhibitions all over the world. He kept Erin's hand in his left one as he held Chelsea's in his right, aware that they looked like a family and pleased they gave that appearance. He was absurdly proud of both Erin and Chelsea.

One enormous hangar had been cleared for a crafts show sponsored by the Officers' Wives Club. Brett, Erin and Chelsea strolled from booth to booth, examining the handmade wares. One woman displayed handmade doll clothes just the right size for Chelsea's Belle. To Chelsea's delight, Brett bought her an entire wardrobe.

"You're spoiling her," Erin murmured, frowning as Brett handed over the money.

"I know," he acknowledged ruefully. "But look at her. How do you resist that?"

Erin's expression softened at the pleasure shining in her daughter's dark eyes. "It isn't easy," she admitted. "But you really should stop. It's not good for her to be so indulged."

Brett wasn't convinced. What could be so bad about making a kid happy? Still, he promised Erin he wouldn't buy anything more. Fortunately, Chelsea didn't see anything else she particularly wanted, which meant that Brett's willpower wasn't put to a test.

It was almost time for the air show to begin when they left the hangar. Brett noticed that a lot of people had brought lawn chairs. Since he hadn't thought of that, he found a small cleared patch of pavement where he and Erin could sit Indian-style, with Chelsea perched on Brett's knee.

Brett hadn't thought to warn the child that the Thunderbirds would be very loud. When the first plane roared over their heads from behind in a crowd-delighting surprise appearance, Chelsea squealed in fright and turned to hide her face in Brett's shoulder, sobbing pitifully.

"Hey, it's okay, baby. It's just an airplane," he reassured her, holding her close and patting her back. He noticed that Erin had instinctively reached out to her daughter, but he didn't release the little girl who'd thrown her arms around his neck and buried her face in his throat. He was stunned by the sense of protectiveness he felt in response to her trembling, the tenderness her vulnerability brought out in him.

He continued to murmur words of comfort until Chelsea had grown accustomed to the noise and turned to watch, though she continued to cling to him for the duration of the earsplitting demonstration. Catching a glimpse of Erin's expression, Brett realized belatedly that she wasn't used to sharing Chelsea in this way. She obviously wasn't quite sure how she felt about having her usual position as comforter usurped by someone else. He wanted her to be comfortable with his relationship with Chelsea. He intended to be a part of the rest of their lives.

They had dinner at a family seafood restaurant in North Little Rock. Then they returned to Erin's house, where Brett waited in the living room, watching a television program while Erin bathed Chelsea and got her ready for bed. At a noise from the doorway, he looked up to find them standing hand in hand, Erin still in her jeans and sweater, Chelsea freshly scrubbed and clad in a lace-trimmed white nightgown. Looking at the dark-haired, blue-eyed woman and the dark-haired, dark-eyed little girl, Brett fell in love all over again. With both of them.

How could any man want more than this? he asked himself. What a fool Martin had been to walk away. Brett had no intention of being so stupid.

"I came to tell you good-night," Chelsea announced.

Brett grinned and held out his arms. "Well, c'mere, then."

She laughed and threw herself across the room, landing in his lap with a thud. Her chubby arms closed around his neck, her rosy lips smacked against his cheek. "Good night, Brett. Thank you for taking me today and for buying me the airplane and the doll clothes." The speech had obviously been rehearsed with her mother, but sounded convincingly sincere.

Holding her soft, sweet-smelling little body close, Brett found his eyes suddenly misting with unexpected tears. "Good night, Chelsea. Sweet dreams."

His gaze locked with Erin's for a moment. Erin's eyes looked suspiciously bright. Were hers filmed with tears, too?

Chelsea wriggled out of his arms and off his lap. Erin led her from the room. Brett could hear the child chattering down the hallway.

It was time, he told himself, rising from the couch to wander restlessly around the room, trying to build his courage. Time to put his entire future in Erin's hands. *God, please let her say yes!* he prayed, his hands clenching at his sides.

How would he bear it if she said no?

He turned when she came back into the room. She smiled. "She'll probably be asleep in minutes. She couldn't wait to put Belle's new nightgown on and snuggle under the covers with her."

"I'm glad she liked the doll clothes." *Make conversation,* Brett ordered himself. *Be cool. Bring up the subject of marriage gradually so you don't scare her off.*

"Would you like some coffee?" Erin offered, turning toward the kitchen. "It'll just take me a few minutes to make some."

"I love you, Erin. I want you to marry me."

Brett winced in self-disgust the moment the words left his mouth. That certainly hadn't been the way he'd intended to ask, he thought irritably, remembering his plan to introduce the subject gradually. The words had simply left his mouth before he realized he was going to say them.

Judging from the look on Erin's face as she slowly turned to stare at him, his words had been even more startling to her. She looked...stunned, he decided, shoving his hands into his pockets to conceal the way they'd suddenly started to shake.

12

STUNNED was too mild a word to describe her reaction to his proposal. It had, quite literally, been the last thing she'd expected to hear just then. She wasn't even certain she'd heard him correctly.

"Married?" she repeated faintly. "You want to get married?"

Brett's face softened. His smile was spine-melting. "Yes. More than anything I've ever wanted before. I love you."

He loved her. A wave of hot, pure joy rushed through her. Then she forced herself to think rationally. How could she marry a man she'd actually known only two weeks? Risk her future—and, more important, Chelsea's—on a whirlwind courtship? "Brett, I—"

"I know you're going to say it's too soon," he said, forestalling those very words. "But we've known each other for months, Erin. As long as lots of people who decide to marry. Our courtship wasn't a conventional one, perhaps, but it was valid. It was enough to make me fall in love with you before I even saw you."

She locked her hands behind her back. "Brett, a string of telephone calls can't really be considered a courtship. You didn't even know my name for the first couple of months."

"I didn't *need* to know your name," he argued stubbornly. "I knew everything that was important about you."

"You didn't know I had a daughter."

His eyes narrowed. "Only because you deliberately kept that from me. I've dealt with that during the past two weeks. My feelings for you haven't changed."

She took a step toward him, lifting her hand in an almost-imploring gesture. "Brett, you have to understand that I can't give you an answer now, not like this. I have responsibilities. I can't—"

"Not another responsible, mature-adult speech, Erin, please." Shoving his hand through his thick hair, he took a deep breath. "Look, I know I'm impulsive and that worries you. But you needn't worry that I'll ever regret proposing to you. I've thought this out. I know what I want."

"You think you know," she corrected him gently, unwilling to hurt him but determined to make him see reason. How could he expect her to just marry him so spontaneously? A decision like that would have to be given months of thought, of preparation. So much was involved, so much at stake. And he still hadn't had time to come to terms with the demands of parenthood. Chelsea hadn't always been an angel around him during the past two weeks, but he'd seen mostly the good side of parenting. He still had no experience with all that was involved.

"I know," he repeated flatly, his gaze holding hers prisoner. "I may be impulsive, Erin, but I'm not naive, and I'm not stupid. I know it won't always be easy. But I believe we can make it. And I know I want to try. I can learn to be a husband and I can learn to be a father, with your help. It's what I want."

She thought she detected a touch of desperation in his golden-brown eyes and her heart twisted. Couldn't he understand it was for his sake as well as her own that she was hesitating?

Brett took the extra step between them and closed his hands around her forearms, holding her tightly. "Erin, I love you," he said again, tersely. "Just tell me if you feel the same way. I need to know what you really want."

She moistened her lips. Why did he suddenly look so anxious? Didn't he know, hadn't he guessed that she'd loved him from the first time they'd made love, if not before? And, as far as what she wanted . . . She thought of her visit with the optometrist, the rush of jealousy she'd felt at the other woman's happiness in her marriage and pregnancy. Erin wanted those things so badly she could taste them. And yet she was so afraid to reach out for them, so afraid of failing again.

"I—I think I love you," she began cautiously, her eyes focused somewhere in the vicinity of Brett's chin. "But—"

He pulled her closer, with hope flaring in his eyes. "Then, what's holding you back?"

She lifted her gaze to his mouth—his sexy, talented, usually smiling mouth. He wasn't smiling now. "Is there really any reason to rush?" she whispered. "Can't we take our time to make sure—really sure—that this is the right step for us."

He frowned. "The thought of returning home alone is what makes me want to rush. I don't want to be alone anymore."

Erin closed her eyes in a spasm of pain. She'd been on such intimate terms with loneliness. It ripped her heart apart to think of being without Brett now, to picture him alone in Boston, missing her the same way. How she wanted to say yes, to abandon all caution and go away with him. But... "I can't," she whispered achingly. "Brett, I can't."

His fingers clenched convulsively, almost bruisingly. "You're a coward," he accused her, his anger almost, but not quite, concealing the underlying vulnerability. "You're afraid to take risks, afraid to trust, afraid to love. You're not doing yourself *or* Chelsea any favors by hiding you both away, the way you've been doing for the past three years."

Stung, Erin finally looked at him, straight in the eye. "It's easy for you to make those accusations. Easy for you to take risks. You have nothing to lose. I have a little girl who has no one to depend on except her mother. I can't— I won't—risk her security until I'm very sure about what I'm doing."

Brett dropped her arms as if his palms had been scalded, his eyes widening in blatant disbelief. "That is the most arrogant thing I've ever heard you say," he exclaimed. "Nothing to lose? You honestly think I have nothing to lose? You think men can't hurt, can't bleed? You think I like the idea of having you reject me after what we've shared the past two weeks? I am in *love* with you, Erin Spencer, and you could break my heart with very little effort. You don't think I'm taking a risk opening myself up for that kind of pain? Think again, lady."

She reached out to him in agitation, her fingers just brushing his arm. "Brett, I'm sorry. I didn't mean— But you have to understand. I don't know what to do. You have to give me time. If it were just me—if it were only my happiness placed at risk—it would be so much easier for me to give you the answer you want. But I have to think about Chelsea. I have to."

"And you don't trust me to think about her happiness, as well," he added, his voice curiously flat. "You still think I'd do something to hurt that little girl. You're still comparing me to the shallow, aging playboy you married."

"No," she denied. "I know you're not like Martin. I just need time, Brett. Please."

His jaw working, he nodded and half turned away. "All right. I'll give you time. But I have to get back to Boston. I can't wait here, put my life on hold indefinitely, until you decide you can trust me. I'm leaving tomorrow."

"I understand," she whispered, crossing her arms over her aching heart.

"There won't be anyone else," he told her, turning suddenly to stare intently into her tear-filled eyes. "There won't ever be anyone else for me. I'll do whatever I have to do to prove to you that I know what I'm doing, what I'm feeling."

Though she knew she was doing the right thing by waiting until she was very sure before giving him an answer to his proposal, the thought of saying goodbye to him tore her apart. She couldn't bear the thought of not seeing him, not touching him, having him in her life only as a voice on the telephone. Desperately, she pictured her daughter, drawing strength from the image of Chelsea's trusting dark eyes. But still she hurt.

With a thin cry, she stepped into Brett's waiting arms. "Hold me, Brett. Please hold me."

"I'll do more than that," he promised roughly. "I'm going to leave you with a night to remember. Something to think about when we're both alone, both lonely. A taste of what we could have every night if only you trusted me, trusted your own feelings."

His mouth covered hers, hard, his arms going around her as if to chain her to him for eternity. Her own closed around his neck and she held him tightly, trying to pretend she'd never have to let him go.

And they made love over and over, their pleasure edged with the awareness that their hours were numbered. It was dawn when he left, weary, grim-lipped. He'd already told her he hated airport goodbyes, that he would call her the next night from Boston. He stepped into Chelsea's room on his way out, standing by the sleeping child's bed for several long, silent moments while Erin watched from the doorway, wrapped in her robe and her pain. Brett leaned down to brush a kiss across Chelsea's chubby cheek and then turned away as though the contact had hurt him, his hands shoving fiercely into the pockets of his jeans.

Erin's throat tightened, her eyes flooding with tears again. Was it really possible that Brett had learned to care for her daughter as much as he said? That he could adapt to an instant family, to the demands parenthood would place on his previously unrestricted life? She hoped so. Oh, how she hoped so! All she needed, she told herself bracingly, was time to be sure. Time for both of them to be sure.

He held her for a long time at the door, his face buried in her throat. And then he kissed her quickly and turned away, hiding his expression. "I love you, Erin," he muttered, his voice choked, his hand on the door.

He was gone before she could answer. She'd wanted to tell him that she loved him, too. Leaning against the closed door, one hand on its smooth, cold surface, she gave in to confusion and exhaustion—and wept.

BRETT WANDERED around his empty apartment, telling himself he really should get to work, wondering how he was ever going to find the enthusiasm to draw his mythical hero when his own life was in such a shambles. It was hard to lose himself in fantasy when reality kept intruding into his once-fertile imagination.

He stood in his room and stared at his big bed picturing himself and Erin rolling on it. That thought made him groan and pace, restless, painfully frustrated. He paused at the door of the guest room, studying its sterile, professionally done decor, thinking how much prettier it would be with Chelsea's toys scattered on the expensive carpeting. He imagined the silence filled with Erin's soft voice, Chelsea's musical laughter. Just as he'd been imagining those things for the past month, ever since he'd made himself return to his real life, giving Erin the time she'd requested to consider his proposal.

He was alone and he wanted a family. His family. The one he'd found in Arkansas.

He glanced at his watch. It was still early afternoon, but maybe he'd call Erin. He could talk to Chelsea, too. Ask her how she was doing, how preschool was going, what she'd learned in her last dance class. Erin had sent him a picture from the dance recital; Chelsea had looked adorable in her sequins and feathers and tights. He should have been there, he thought for at least the hundredth time. Should have been in the audience with a video camera and a proud smile. And afterward, he could have taken his family out to dinner and then gone home to make love to his wife before drifting into a contented, satisfied sleep.

Dammit, why was Erin denying him those experiences? She was refusing them both the pleasures inherent in marriage and parenthood, just because she didn't trust him to handle the inevitable rocky times. He knew it wasn't all good times and laughter. Knew there'd be days of frustration, of conflict, of tension. Hell, that was all part of it. And he wanted it all.

With sudden decision, he grabbed his coat and headed for the door. He needed to get out, away from the haunted silence, the taunting images. He needed to see people, hear them, watch other families enjoying what he'd been denied—just being together, sharing their lives.

He didn't look at the telephone as he passed it on his way out. This time the cold, plastic instrument couldn't give him what he needed.

LEAVING CHELSEA watching her favorite PBS children's program, Erin drifted into the kitchen, telling herself she needed to put something out to thaw for dinner. She paused, instead, by the telephone, looking longingly at it. It was hours earlier than Brett usually called, and yet she wanted so badly just to hear his voice.

For the past month, her life had revolved around the telephone. She seemed to exist from call to call, going through the motions of working woman and devoted mother during the daytime, fully content only when she was talking to Brett each night. And then she had to amend even that thought. She would never be fully content as long as she and Brett were so far apart. She wanted to see him, wanted to touch him. She wanted him.

She knew he was as miserable as she was. She heard it in his voice every time they spoke. Time and again she'd found herself on the verge of surrender, ready to promise anything he wanted just to end the torment of being without him. Time and again a vision of Chelsea's trusting little face had floated into her mind, stopping the words in her throat. How could she be sure? she asked herself over and over. How could she know she was doing the right thing?

Corey thought she was crazy for putting herself through this. During their last telephone call she'd urged Erin to take a chance at happiness, to fight for what she wanted. After all, Corey had walked away from a successful job and a hectic social life to hide herself away with her art and her books and her own company. She'd assured Erin she'd never regretted that decision, that it was something she'd needed to do to find herself. One couldn't live one's whole life worrying about the consequences of every decision, she lectured. Sometimes a person just had to take a chance.

Adam had said little when Erin had told him about Brett's proposal. This was a decision she had to make on her own, he'd told her reluctantly. He'd been telling her for some time that she needed to find someone, to start living her life again. He couldn't tell her whether Brett would make her happy, couldn't predict the future for her. He only wished he could, to spare her any pain. All he could do was be there if she needed to talk. "Whatever you do," he'd added, "I love you. I'll always be on your side."

Though his words had warmed her, they hadn't been enough. She'd wanted him to tell her what to do. Adam had always seemed so competent, so infallible. Why couldn't he tell her what to do now? For the first time in years, she just wanted to let someone else make the decisions, someone else worry about the consequences.

She wanted to be with Brett. She wanted to do what was right for her daughter. She wanted to crawl into bed and pull the covers over her head.

Sighing, she reached for the phone. She really needed to talk to Brett.

He wasn't home. She let the phone ring for a long time before she finally gave up and replaced her receiver. He'd obviously forgotten to turn on his answering machine. She wasn't sure what she would have said if he had.

HE CALLED AT HIS USUAL time, around ten. Erin had been waiting for the call ever since she'd tucked Chelsea into bed two hours earlier. Drawing her knees up to hug them with her free arm, she sat on the bed, the telephone cradled to her ear. "I tried to call you earlier," she told Brett almost immediately.

"Did you? I was out."

"Yes, I know." She didn't ask where he'd been, though she would have liked to. She trusted him, of course. But she really would have liked to ask.

"So, what have you been doing?" Brett asked, stiltedly making conversation.

"Just the usual," she answered with a shrug she knew he couldn't see. "I finished my assignments for Redding & Howard today. I should be getting some more next week. How about you? Will you make your first-of-the-month deadline?"

"Maybe," he answered rather grimly. "By some miracle."

She was instantly concerned. "You're having trouble working?"

"Don't worry about it. It happens sometimes. Is Chelsea asleep?"

"Yes."

"Thanks for sending me the pictures of her dance recital. She looked really cute. I wish I'd seen her."

"I wish you had, too," Erin murmured, remembering how empty the chair next to her had seemed that evening.

"I miss you, Erin."

He always told her, always sounded so sincere. Yet tonight there was a new intensity in the quietly spoken words, a trace of despair. Erin's heart twisted. "I miss you, too, Brett."

"All I have to do is close my eyes and I can see you. Sometimes I can see you so clearly that I can almost reach out and touch you. Almost. It's not enough."

"No." She closed her eyes.

"I want you," he said starkly. "So much I hurt. I go to sleep hurting and I wake up the same way. I want you in bed beneath me. I want to kiss you, to touch you. I want to feel your breasts against my chest, your legs wrapped around mine. I want to be inside you, loving you, hearing the little sounds you make when you come."

Erin moaned. "Brett, please. Don't."

"Do you want me, Erin? Does your body tremble for my touch? Are your breasts aching, hungry for my hands, my mouth?"

"Yes," she breathed, her aroused nipples brushing almost painfully against the fabric of her nightgown. She hugged her knees more tightly, trying to ease the discomfort. The pressure only made it worse.

"I want to kiss them. I want to take you into my mouth and feel you arch against me. I want to run my hand up your soft thigh and slide my fingers between your legs. You're already hot and wet for me, aren't you, Erin?"

Her eyes tightly closed, she squeezed her thighs together, almost whimpering at the moist, pulsing emptiness between them. She tried to beg him to stop but she couldn't speak. Her breath came fast and ragged, escaping her lips in a gasp of need.

Brett's voice was raw, gritty. "All I have to do is think of you and I get hard. Cold showers don't help. Exercise doesn't help. I can't concentrate on anything else to make the ache go away. I need you."

"Brett—" His name was little more than a sob.

"The calls aren't enough now. Not since we've been together, not now that I know how incredible we are together. I need to be with you. How much longer are you going to torture both of us by keeping us apart?"

"I don't—"

"Come to Boston, Erin. Please."

Tears welled in her eyes and began to cascade down her cheeks. "I can't."

His sigh was weary, heartrendingly dispirited. "Maybe I'd better go," he said heavily. "I'm not feeling quite in control tonight. I'm only going to make us both miserable, say something I'll probably regret. I'll talk to you tomorrow, all right?"

She was still struggling to control her breathing. She clutched the receiver so tightly her hand cramped. Finally she swallowed and murmured, "Yes."

"I love you, Erin."

The hoarse murmur brought fresh tears to her closed eyes. "Good night, Brett," she whispered, then quickly dropped the receiver into its cradle. She wrapped both arms around her raised legs and rested her face on her knees, her tears soaking through the thin nightgown. Her body throbbed with need and her heart ached until she thought it would shatter. Her breasts were swollen so tight they hurt, aroused by nothing more than Brett's words.

How much longer could they go on like this? How long until one or both of them broke?

Why couldn't someone tell her what to do?

BRETT SLAMMED his phone down and rolled onto his side on his big, empty bed, cursing himself for starting something he couldn't finish. His blood pounded heavily in his veins, his breath sharp-edged as it slashed in and out of his lungs. His hand brushed that part of him that was so painfully, throbbingly swollen and he dully considered easing the ache in the only way available to him at the moment. He refrained because he couldn't bear the thought of the heart-deep emptiness afterward.

He couldn't go on this way much longer. He needed Erin, loved her until he was half sick with it. If this was his penalty for living on his own terms for so long, then he had surely paid in full for every selfish, irresponsible action.

A hundred times he'd told himself to go after her, stay on her heels until she couldn't run any farther. A hundred times he'd told himself that the only chance he had of winning her was to wait for her to come to him.

He buried his face in the pillow, his fist clenched at his side, willing his body to cool. Something had to give, he thought again. Soon.

He could only hope it wouldn't be his sanity.

IT WAS THREE in the morning when Erin reached again for the phone. She hadn't slept, hadn't been able to do anything except lie on her back in the darkness and stare at the ceiling as if hoping to find the answers there to all her questions. She didn't stop to think that it was an hour later in Boston, that the middle of the night wasn't the time to make calls. The phone rang twice on the other end and then Brett answered, his voice sleep-thick and disoriented. "Yeah? What?"

"I'll marry you, Brett. If you're sure it's what you want, I'll marry you." Even as she said the words, Erin prayed that the decision was the right one—for her, for Chelsea, for Brett. She only knew she'd never be truly happy again unless she took this chance.

A long, stunned pause followed her announcement. And then Brett spoke again, tentatively. "Erin?"

She couldn't help smiling through her tears. "You've proposed to someone else?"

"Wait a minute." She could hear bedsprings creaking quietly, the rustle of fabric. She closed her eyes and pictured him, sleep tousled and heavy eyed, wearing nothing but his oh-so-sexy smile. "Okay, I'm awake," he told her clearly. "Now, say it again."

"I'll marry you," she repeated obediently.

His laugh was quick, breathless. "That's what I thought you said. God, I hope this isn't a dream."

"You're not dreaming."

"How soon can you get here?"

"You want me to come there?" she asked, her fingers nervously pleating the sheet that covered her. She thought wistfully of the state she'd grown up in, that she loved so dearly. Could she really be happy in Boston?

She only knew she couldn't be happy without Brett, wherever they chose to live.

"Yeah. I want to show you around, see how you like it. We've got a thousand plans to make and I want to do it together. In person. You'll stay here, of course. There's an extra bedroom for Chelsea."

"You want me to bring Chelsea?"

"Of course, I want you to bring Chelsea," he answered impatiently. "Did you think I'd ask you to leave her behind? We're going to be a family, Erin. The three of us. The sooner we start, the better. So, when can you be here?"

"How soon do you want us?" she asked, clinging tightly to her courage.

"Now," he answered promptly.

She smiled. "How about later in the week?"

He sighed. "I guess I can wait that long. Barely. I'll be working my buns off in the meantime to clear some free time for us."

"I'll get things together here, then. I'll let you know when we'll be there."

"I'll send you the tickets."

"That's not necessary."

"I'll send you the tickets," he repeated firmly.

She knew when to give in. "All right."

"Erin?"

"Yes, Brett?"

"I love you."

"I love you, too," she whispered. *God, please let me be doing the right thing.*

THINGS STARTED GOING wrong almost as soon as the airplane took off from the Little Rock Regional Airport, headed for Memphis. Originally excited about her first plane ride, Chelsea was frightened by the sounds and movements of takeoff. Her ears hurt from the changing altitude and she was too young to know how to relieve the pressure herself. Tearfully, she accepted the bubble gum Erin had brought for that purpose, huddling into her seat with Belle and chewing fiercely.

Chelsea had just gotten used to her surroundings when it was time to change planes. She sobbed through the second takeoff, despite Erin's crooning comfort. She was finally distracted when the stewardesses served lunch. Intrigued by the novelty of being served in her seat on the fold-down tray, Chelsea grew much more cheerful, even eating nearly every bite on her plastic plate.

Erin, on the other hand, could hardly touch her meal. She was tormented by doubts and questions. Had she done the right thing? Would Brett adjust to having his bachelor home invaded by her and her child? Would she ever be comfortable in Boston after living all her life in Arkansas? Would she fit in? Would Brett be ashamed of her provincial ways?

What about the crime rate she'd read about? The violence? The pollution? Wouldn't it be better to raise Chelsea in the less stressful, less urbanized atmosphere of North Little Rock?

Was she doing the right thing?

Brett was waiting at the airport. He hardly allowed them to step through the gate before catching Erin in his arms for a welcoming kiss that nearly singed her eyelashes. She was bruised and breathless when he released her to sweep Chelsea into his arms for a less powerful, but equally enthusiastic hug. He'd bought flowers for Erin, an adorable stuffed monkey for Chelsea.

Tired and overly excited by the trip, Chelsea was very quiet during the ride across Boston to Brett's town-house apartment. Erin was having trouble, herself, finding things to say. Even Brett's broad smile had begun to dim by the time they arrived. He and Erin exchanged long, grave looks when he opened the front door, saying, "Welcome home."

Chelsea immediately ran inside to investigate. Erin was as impressed as her daughter by the lovely decor. Brett's apartment had been furnished in a contemporary style that was quite comfortable looking despite its modernness. He gave them a tour, showing them the state-of-the-art kitchen, the spacious dining room and living room, and his office.

Chelsea seemed fascinated by the oversize comic-book drawings littering his desk and drawing board. "You're welcome to look at them when I'm with you," Brett told the child. "But don't touch, okay? This is almost a month's work."

"I don't want you in this room without me or Brett, Chelsea. Understand?" Erin added to reinforce Brett's mild warning. He probably wasn't aware that understatement had little effect on an almost-four-year-old, she thought with nervous amusement.

The next stop on the tour was the master bedroom. His eyes on Erin, Brett set her bags at the foot of the bed. "Do you like it?" he asked quietly.

She looked from him to the enormous bed, refusing to even consider how many other women might have shared it with him. "It's a lovely room," she replied firmly. "It looks quite comfortable."

His grin conveyed a masculine confidence. "I think you'll enjoy it."

She flushed and turned away.

"And this, Chelsea, is your room," Brett announced, opening the door to the guest room. "What do you think?"

Chelsea looked around the strange room with its trendy adult furnishings, then turned uncertainly to Erin. "It doesn't look like my room," she declared.

"It will when we bring all your things here," Erin assured her. She'd been trying to prepare the child for the upcoming move, though she'd wondered if she should have waited until a definite date had been set. And then she'd told herself that Chelsea should be included from the beginning in the plans Erin and Brett were making. After all, this marriage would affect the rest of Chelsea's life, too.

"So—um—would you like to freshen up or anything? I have reservations at a new restaurant for dinner, but I thought we could look around Boston a little first, if you like."

"That sounds fine," Erin responded. "Doesn't it, Chelsea?"

Clinging to her doll and her mother's hand, Chelsea nodded gravely. "Yes."

Brett cleared his throat loudly and made an awkward motion toward the door. "Let's go, then. I'm sure you'll really love my town."

13

BOSTON WAS BIG. And busy. And crowded. Erin couldn't help feeling dwarfed by the buildings towering over her head as they drove down a bustling street. Downtown Little Rock wasn't this crowded and hectic even at rush hour, and the sky-touching towers at home were spaced several blocks apart rather than side by side. She and Chelsea huddled into their coats, unaccustomed to the cold—it was still comfortably warm at home.

Chelsea stared around her silently, not at all impressed by the historic sights. Erin was surprised at the age of some of the sites Brett pointed out. Arkansas, of course, had still been inhabited by Native Americans when some of these places were built. She spent a lot of time trying to understand the rapid, flat-voweled speech patterns of the people around her, and was painfully aware of her own slower, obviously Southern accent.

"What do you think, so far?" Brett questioned, holding her hand and searching her face with his anxious gaze.

Even Brett sounded different here, she noticed with a hard swallow, hearing the way he unconsciously dropped the *r* in *far*. "It's a lot different from home," she admitted with a weak smile.

"I suppose it seems that way at first. I hope you'll learn to love it here, as I have," he said, glancing around with an almost-proprietary air. Erin could tell that he really loved his adopted city. She hoped he was right about her growing to love it, too.

"Erin." As if reading the doubts in her eyes, Brett tightened his fingers around hers. "If you don't like it here, if you decide it's not right for us, we'll move. We'll find someplace where you can be comfortable raising our children. Just give it a chance, okay?"

Bemused by his mention of their children, Erin smiled shakily and nodded. "I will. I promise."

He pulled her close for a quick kiss. "I'm not sure I can wait until Chelsea goes to bed tonight," he murmured. "It's been so long since I've held you properly."

Her knees already weakening in anticipation of the night, she clung to him for a moment, until Chelsea demanded her attention. She gave Brett a quick smile of promise before turning to answer her daughter's question.

FROM THE TIME they arrived at the popular new Cambridge restaurant, it was glaringly apparent that Brett wasn't accustomed to including a young child in his evening plans. It wasn't a family restaurant. The snooty hostess rolled her eyes in poorly veiled annoyance at having to find accommodations for a small child. She finally produced a booster seat with the air of someone who'd had to look long and hard for the distasteful item. Erin's cheeks were warm when she settled Chelsea in the seat, aware of the surreptitious looks from other diners, all of whom looked like trendy, upwardly-mobile types who hadn't yet scheduled children into their lives.

An equally snooty waitress offered to take their drink orders. Intimidated by the woman's hauteur, Erin asked for water. The woman sighed and asked, "What brand?"

Since she didn't think she should answer "Tap," Erin named the first brand she could remember, hoping it was still in vogue. "With a twist of lime," she added, trying to appear more sophisticated than she felt at the moment.

Giving Erin a faint smile, Brett ordered a drink, then asked Chelsea what she'd like. "Chocolate milk," the child answered promptly.

The waitress sighed noisily. "We don't *do* chocolate milk," she grumbled, obviously irritated. "We probably have regular."

"That will be fine," Erin replied hastily.

Brett waited until the woman was out of hearing before chuckling. "She's a real sweetheart, huh? Sorry, Erin, I had no idea the service here was so lousy."

She managed a smile and told him not to worry about it.

The meal went downhill from there. The Waitress from Hell obviously didn't approve of Erin's order, could hardly hide her disbelief at Chelsea's request, and was marginally pleasant to Brett only because she seemed to sense he belonged there. Erin was feeling more and more out of place. Maybe she should have stayed in Arkansas, she thought miserably. She and Chelsea could be eating at a McDonald's or Bonanza or Po'Folks restaurant.

The seemingly interminable meal finally drew to an end—but only after Chelsea had become so uncomfortable in the tense atmosphere that she began to whine. Erin drew a deep breath of relief when they were finally in Brett's car.

"I'm sorry," he said again, shaking his head in disgust. "What a terrible place. I'd never been there before, and I had no idea it was one of those joints so impressed by its own image that patrons are treated like interlopers. I'll never go back."

"You couldn't have known how they felt about children," Erin responded, trying to reassure him. "I suppose having a child around cramps your style a little."

He pulled his brows downward in obvious annoyance. "Don't be ridiculous. It wasn't Chelsea's fault the staff was so obnoxious. Next time, I'll ask some of my married friends to recommend a child-friendly place to eat."

Though she was so tired her head drooped pitifully, Chelsea didn't want to go to bed in the strange bedroom alone. Erin lay down beside her until the child finally dropped off, her doll clutched tightly in her arms. And then Erin slipped from the bed and tiptoed out of the room.

Brett waited for her in the den, his eyes shadowy. "I guess you've had more enjoyable days."

She didn't want him to blame himself. "Maybe we just tried to do too much at once," she suggested. "Chelsea and I were both tired from the trip."

"Tomorrow will be better," he reassured, and she wondered which of them he was trying to convince.

"I'm sure you're right," she replied, wanting to believe it herself.

He stepped closer to her and cupped her face between his hands. She covered them with her own. "I've missed you so much," he murmured, his thumb tracing her trembling lower lip. "I've wanted you here for so long. It's going to work out, Erin. I promise you that."

"I know," she whispered, searching his golden-brown eyes for any sign of doubt. She found none. Brett truly believed that they were doing the right thing. She smiled and touched the tip of her tongue to his thumb.

He groaned and tugged her closer, covering her mouth with his. "God, I want you," he muttered against her lips. "I'm going crazy with it."

She kissed him lingeringly, then stepped back to hold out her hand to him. "What are you waiting for?" she urged quietly.

Smiling, he took her hand, his fingers squeezing hers tightly as he led her to the master bedroom.

Quickly abandoning their clothes, they tumbled onto the big bed. Their hands sought out intimately remembered territory, their mouths clinging, tongues dueling. They couldn't linger to savor slowly the first time in so many weeks. Their coupling was hot and frantic. Erin peaked almost immediately when he thrust into her. Brett wasn't far behind. Their muffled cries mingled, their harsh breathing echoing in the shadowy corners of the room.

And then they began again. This time they lingered. And savored. This time they climaxed together in deep, blissful, seemingly endless swells.

"I love you," Brett repeated again and again, his hand stroking her damp, trembling flesh as he calmed her afterward. He still found it hard to believe she was actually here with him, as he'd imagined it so many times. "I love you so much."

She turned her face into his sweat-beaded shoulder, tasting his warm, salty skin. "I love you."

"I want to get married soon. I want to adopt Chelsea and make another baby for her to play with. Okay with you?"

She lifted her head with an effort, obviously surprised. "You want to adopt her?"

He answered her very seriously. "Yes. I've thought about it a lot. I want us all to have the same name, be a real family. I want to be her father, not her stepfather. I want her to call me Daddy. If she wants to, of course," he added a bit less certainly.

"I think she'd like that," Erin murmured, her voice sounding suspiciously thick. "She's always wanted a daddy."

"I'll be a good one, Erin. I promise."

"I know you will," she whispered, fighting tears. "Oh, Brett."

He wasn't quite finished. "I want you to tell Martin to take his child-support checks and spend them on his latest jail-bait girlfriend. Chelsea doesn't need anything from him."

Erin smiled. He knew she'd been anticipating that call for a very long time. "All right."

Answering her smile with a deeply sensual one of his own, Brett reached for her again. "Erin—"

"*Mommy!*"

Erin sighed and reached for his robe, which he'd left across the foot of the bed that morning. "I may be a while," she warned him.

"I could go to her," he offered, surprising both of them.

She shook her head quickly. "No. I'll take care of her. You rest."

He watched her hurry from the room in response to another cry. And he realized that she was still uncertain about his role in her daughter's life. That she still wasn't totally convinced he was ready for the responsibilities of parenthood. It hurt, but he was determined to prove her wrong—no matter what he had to do to convince her.

FOR THE NEXT THREE DAYS Brett dedicated himself to entertaining Erin and Chelsea. He and Erin discussed their wedding plans, deciding to fly back to Arkansas to be married so that his sister and her friends and brother could attend. Brett would make arrangements for his parents to be flown there for the ceremony. They would leave the following week, after Brett had mailed his next comic-book installments. They'd spend another week making arrangements to sell Erin's house and ship her things to Boston. And then they'd be married in the little church she'd attended most of her life.

Erin called her minister from Boston, and was pleased that he'd be able to work them into his schedule on the date they requested. Even Adam promised to attend, telling Erin he was sure she had made the right decision this time. She sounded happier, he told her, than she had in a very long time.

Things seemed to be working out very well, indeed.

Brett went out of his way to find things to do that Chelsea would enjoy. She loved the harbor area, particularly the aquarium. They spent hours there. He took her to a toy store and bought her an armload of playthings. He bought her clothes from the trendiest children's store he could find, decking her out like a little model. Chelsea was blissful, her every whim satisfied. Brett asked her how she felt about calling him "Daddy." Chelsea agreed that she'd like that very much—especially when she discovered that Brett couldn't bring himself to deny her anything whenever she used that particular word.

Erin began to worry. "You're spoiling her, Brett. Believe me, you're going to regret it."

He only smiled. "C'mon, Erin, I've never had a kid to spoil before. What could be the harm?"

"The harm," she answered seriously, "is in having her expect you to give her whatever she wants. That isn't always possible, you know, or even preferable. A child needs limits. You're letting her get away with murder. You don't even want me to discipline her."

He shrugged. "She really hasn't done anything that needed disciplining. She's a very good little girl, Erin."

"I know," Erin admitted, softening reluctantly at his praise of her daughter's behavior. "But, please, Brett, trust me to know what's best for her."

Brett frowned. She knew he was trying very hard to demonstrate that he'd be a good father, and that touched her. But she worried about what would happen when he tired of pampering Chelsea; when he realized that he'd created a tiny monster. It was becoming harder for Erin to balance Brett's indulgence. Blessed with every child's innate talent for manipulation, Chelsea knew she had only to turn to Brett for whatever she wanted.

They were spending a quiet afternoon at home when the crisis occurred.

Brett and Erin sat in the den, making lists of things that had to be done before their wedding, immersed in details. The last time they'd checked, Chelsea had been happily playing in her room with some of her many new toys. It was Erin who realized that the child had been too quiet for a bit too long. "I'd better make sure she's still playing," she announced, uncoiling her legs from beneath her to stretch lazily.

Catching a glimpse of smooth, silky skin when her sweater lifted an inch from the waistband of her slacks, Brett couldn't resist reaching out to touch. "Maybe she's taking a nap," he suggested hopefully, thinking of the delightful ways they could spend an hour or so of privacy.

Erin gave him a look that mocked his optimism. "Yeah, sure," she murmured, catching his hand in its sneaky foray and returning it firmly to his knee. "I'll be back in a minute."

She'd been gone less than that when he heard her calling Chelsea. "What's wrong?" he called out.

"I can't find her," she answered, appearing in the doorway with a frown of concern. "She's not in her room. I'll check our room."

Brett pushed himself off the couch to join the search, smiling faintly at Erin's words. "'Our room,'" she'd said. He really liked the sound of that. It sounded so—so settled. Permanent. Married.

Yeah, he liked that a lot.

And then he turned his thoughts to Chelsea's possible whereabouts. Where was she? What was she getting into that was keeping her so suspiciously quiet? Some nagging instinct made him check his office first.

The bellow escaped him before he could hold it back. *"Chelsea!"*

Starting guiltily, Chelsea looked up from his desk, her hand still clutching a red felt-tip marker. Before her lay nearly a month's work. Or, rather, the remains of nearly a month's work, now liberally smeared with bright red ink. "I wanted to color the pictures," Chelsea told him warily, her dark eyes widening in response to his expression.

Torn between anguish and fury, Brett studied the results of her mischief. *Ruined,* he thought grimly. It would take him at least a week of sixteen-hour days to make his deadline now. "Chelsea, didn't I tell you to stay out of here?" he demanded, his hands clenched at his hips as he glared at the little girl huddled in his chair. He really couldn't remember the last time he'd been this angry. With anyone.

"Yes, sir," she replied. "But, Daddy, I wanted to color," she added, tilting her chin up and looking at him the way she had every time she'd wanted anything during the past few days, he realized sickly. And he'd given her whatever she'd wanted, then. She had no reason to expect him to set limits now.

Hearing a choked groan from the doorway, he turned to find Erin standing there, her face stricken as she took in what had happened. "Oh, Brett, I'm sorry."

He drew a deep breath and made a gesture he intended to mean that he was turning the situation over to her. But, though he could tell she was holding herself back with the greatest effort, she didn't move. She only looked at him with an expression that said quite clearly, *You wanted to be a father. Now's the time to start.*

I can't! he thought in panic, trying to convey the message with his eyes as Chelsea watched intently. *I don't know how to do this!*

Erin only waited, watching him steadily.

She trusted him, he realized abruptly, staggeringly. She trusted him to deal with her daughter, despite his obvious anger with the child. And he'd never felt more helpless in his life. What did he know about disciplining children? What if he screwed up? What if he ruined the kid's life?

Turning slowly to Chelsea, he tried to remember what his own father would have done. That wasn't hard. His dad would have tanned his hide but good. Though he'd never doubted his father's love and concern, Brett wasn't about to resort to that. Instead, he relied on carefully selected words spoken in a low, serious tone.

"I'm very angry with you, Chelsea. I asked you not to touch these. I told you how important these papers were. And now you've scribbled on them and I'll have to work very hard to redo them."

Chelsea's lower lip trembled. "But I wanted to color," she repeated, as if that explained everything.

"I bought you two new coloring books," he replied evenly. "You should have colored in those."

Her enormous brown eyes filled touchingly with tears. "Are you going to spank me?"

"No," he answered. "But I think you'd better go to your room while I clean this up. Sit on the bed and don't play with your toys, understand? I want you to think about how you'd feel if someone tore up something very important to you. We'll talk about that when I finish in here."

She sniffed and nodded, tears rolling copiously down her pink cheeks. Dragging her feet, she headed for the door, risking one peek at her mother, who stood with arms folded, brows drawn into a reproving frown. And then she paused to look up at Brett. "Do you still like me?" she asked, her little voice just barely audible.

He melted, though he did his best to conceal it. Trying to keep his voice even, he said, "Chelsea, I love you. Very much. Just because I'm angry with you doesn't mean I love you any less. You're probably going to be mad at me at times. That's what happens in a family. And it's important that we learn to respect each other's property. Do you understand?"

Her brow crinkling, Chelsea nodded. "I have to leave your stuff alone."

He fought the beginnings of a smile. "Yeah. Unless you ask permission first and unless I tell you it's okay, you have to leave my stuff alone."

"Come on, Chelsea. We're going to your room. Now," Erin added, taking her daughter's shoulder in a gentle, though firm grip. She glanced briefly at Brett as she led the child from the room.

Brett tried to decide what that look had meant. Did she disapprove of the way he'd handled the situation? Had he been firm enough? Maybe he'd been too firm. Maybe he shouldn't have told Chelsea that he was angry with her. Maybe he shouldn't have ordered her to her room. Maybe he should have just shrugged the whole thing off and complimented her on her artistic talent. What if he'd traumatized her so severely that he'd stifled all her budding creativity.

Sighing in self-disgust, he began to gather his ruined pages. Surely he'd done the right thing. After all, Chelsea had to learn that his work was off-limits. He was certain that Erin would never allow her daughter to get away with destroying assignments she did for the Little Rock advertising agency. Chelsea had simply gotten spoiled, and it was past time he persuaded her that couldn't go on.

He hoped he'd done the right thing.

"What's the damage?" Erin asked quietly from the other side of the desk.

He hadn't heard her come back in. He looked up slowly, trying to read her expression. All he could detect was concern as she anxiously examined his desk. "It's not as bad as it looked at first," he replied. "But it may put our trip to Arkansas back a few days. The wedding's still on as planned, but we won't have quite as long beforehand to get your things in order, I'm afraid. And I guess our sight-seeing trips are over for the time being. I'm going to have to concentrate on redoing these pages so I can get them to my publisher in time."

"I understand," Erin assured him. "Chelsea and I will do everything we can to help you. We'll stay out of your way while you're working. In fact, maybe we should go on home and I can be taking care of things there while you—"

"No," Brett cut in quickly. "I don't want you to go back without me."

"Now, Brett, be reasonable. We'd only be in your way here and I have a thousand things I could be doing at home. There's no reason for us to stay."

"Erin, I'm not going to stop working after we're married. I can work with you and Chelsea here."

"I know you can. I'll make sure of that after we're married," she answered with a smile. "But this time I think it would be best if I take care of things in Arkansas while you're doing this. It will give us much more free time for each other after the wedding," she said, supplying the one argument to which he couldn't object.

He capitulated, as she knew he would. "All right. But I'll miss you. I'll resent every minute that we're apart."

"I know. So will I. But it won't be long," she promised. "Soon we'll be together for always. No more separations."

"I like the sound of that."

She smiled. "So do I."

His own weak smile faded. "Erin, did I—I mean, was I okay? Was I too hard on her? Should I have—?"

She advanced steadily around the desk, her loving gaze locked with his. "Brett . . . Darling. You are an excellent father. You're exactly the kind of father I always wanted for Chelsea. You're loving and kind and funny and sweet. And you were wonderful today. You'll make mistakes sometimes—God knows, I've made my share and will make more—but that's all part of it. We can only follow our instincts and hope for the best."

He almost sagged in relief. "Thank you for trusting me, Erin. I know how hard it was for you."

She cupped his face in her hand and leaned toward him to brush her lips across his. "When it came right down to it, it wasn't hard at all," she murmured. "It was probably the easiest thing I've ever done. I love you, Brett."

He pulled her into his arms, burying his face in her throat. "I love you. Oh, Erin, I love you so much. How did I ever survive without you?"

She laughed quietly and sought his mouth for another kiss. He kissed her eagerly, telling himself that he had to be the luckiest man on earth. He'd found a beautiful, witty, loving wife and an adorable, if normally mischievous daughter—all because he'd once pressed the wrong button on his telephone.

Only it hadn't been the wrong number, after all, he reflected with a surge of satisfaction.

It had been the right number all along.

Epilogue

HER STILL-SLIGHTLY-DAMP body wrapped in a thick terry robe, Erin stepped out of the bathroom, toweling her wet hair. The telephone on the bedside table rang, startling her. One brow lifted as she answered it, looking around the room with a frown. "Hello?"

"Oh, excuse me," a deep voice said. "I was trying to call my sister."

Smiling, Erin shook her head in amused exasperation. Now she knew why the elegant hotel room had been deserted when she'd finished her shower. "I'm sorry, you must have the wrong number," she replied, playing along with his whimsical game. "But you sound very nice. I'd like to meet you sometime."

"Gee, I don't know. What if it didn't work out?"

"Oh, I have a feeling it will work out," she responded in a sultry voice.

"In that case, why don't we get married?"

"I think we already did," she answered with a grin, smugly examining her shiny new gold band. "Five hours ago, to be exact."

"Then what am I doing in the hotel lobby?"

"That's what I'd like to know."

"I'm on my way," he promised her.

"Hurry," she urged, letting the terry robe fall to the floor. "I've learned not to waste precious time." And she gently hung up the phone. She stood where she was, waiting for him, happily anticipating the night ahead of them. Chelsea was staying with Brett's sister and her doting new cousins. Brett and Erin had three whole days ahead of them. Alone. Just the two of them.

She was sure they'd make excellent use of those three days—and nights.

He was there in a matter of minutes, sweeping her into his arms with a broad grin. "Relationships are so much nicer in the flesh," he observed, his hands stroking her bare skin as he pulled her closer to his already aroused body.

"Yes, they are," she agreed, lifting her hands to unfasten the buttons of his shirt.

They tumbled together onto the bed, laughing breathlessly as they rushed to rid Brett of his decidedly unnecessary clothing. And then they began an all-night celebration of the odd whims of fate.